# RUINED TRILOGY

*To Paige, who always answers my crime texts at 3am and never asks questions. ILY! And to Violet. Thank you for your help and your friendship.*

# *About the Book*

**One look at his curvy captive and this Mafia boss will risk it all. Even if it means toppling his own kingdom to the ground.**

### Rafe Valentino

A life in chains was the deal I made with my father to win my twin's freedom.

My soul is black with the things I've done to keep my promise.

I never regretted any of it until now. Until *her*.

Amalia Santiago's bravado and fierce defiance make me feel alive in a way I never expected.

I was never meant to fall for her.

I don't deserve to put my filthy hands all over her pristine body.

She's supposed to be my prisoner.

But now, she may be my downfall instead.

### Amalia Santiago

When the devil came for my foster brother, I let him take me in his place.

I swore I'd find a way out of this mess for both of us.

Except Rafe Valentino wasn't supposed to have a heart...

And I wasn't supposed to fall for the ruthless crime boss.

So why do I come alive when he touches me?

Now, I'm one wrong move away from destroying everything.

And *nothing* is what it seems.

How do I sacrifice the man I love to save my brother?

If you enjoy OTT possessive older men with a little bit of darkness in them and sassy, curvy heroines with heart, get ready to fall for Rafe and Amalia in this sweet and extra steamy romance. As always, Nichole Rose books come complete with a guaranteed HEA.

# Contents

The quiet scratching on my bedroom door brings me fully awake. My heart thuds against my breastbone, jarring my senses. For a moment, I think I dreamed the noise. And then I hear the bone-chilling sound again.

This is no dream.

Someone is inside my apartment.

I slip my shaking hand between my bed and my nightstand, feeling for the small bat I keep hidden there. As a woman alone in Chicago, one can never be too careful. I learned that lesson early. My foster brother, Diego Butera, made sure I did. He and my foster father, Alvise, drilled it into my head before I even learned my multiplication tables.

My hand closes around the handle of the bat. I grit my teeth, holding my breath when the cool wood jostles against the metal bedframe. If whoever is trying to get into my room hears the faint noise, they don't sound the alarm.

1

I send up a prayer, hoping that means there's only one intruder.

The scratching comes again.

I carefully pull the bat up onto the bed with me and then sit upright. I move slowly, trying to keep whoever is out there from hearing me. If they know I'm awake, I lose the element of surprise, and it's the only thing I've got on my side right now.

Whoever they are, they're not trying to get into my bedroom for the fun of it. If they wanted to rob me, they could have taken my stuff and left already. No, that's not what they're here for.

Did they find out who I am? No. How could they? I haven't been *her* since I was ten years old.

Diego.

*What did you do, Diego?*

I love my brother. He's the only family I have since Alvise died when I was a teenager. But Diego is... complicated. He's been playing both sides of the law for so long, I'm no longer sure if he knows which side he's actually on. He clawed his way out of the streets, only to fall right back into them as soon as the ink dried on his law degree. Isn't that usually how it goes in places like this?

You can take the boy out of the streets, but you can't take the streets out of the boy. Especially when La Cosa Nostra is involved. They may play a more sophisticated game, but at the end of the day, they're a gang just like the rest. Blood in, blood out. That's how the saying goes, isn't it?

He was never really out anyway. Not entirely. This

world calls to him just like it did his biological father. The mafia is in his blood. He'll never be free. Not so long as the man who killed his father still breathes. He wants vengeance too badly.

Diego's been working toward that goal for as long as I've known him. Every step he takes moves him a little bit closer. He'll succeed...or he'll die trying. There is no changing his mind. I know because I've tried. He wants vengeance. And I want out so badly I can taste it.

But I won't leave him here alone. I can't.

I creep from the bed, tiptoeing across the plush carpet with the bat clutched firmly in my hands. I place my feet carefully, my eyes picking out a path across my room in the moonlight trickling in from the windows. It's not much light, barely enough to turn my furniture into thick, shadowy blotches in the dark. But I've walked this same stretch of carpeting often enough to wear it thin, trying to outpace the night.

The doorknob rattles, turning slowly.

I scurry the last few feet, cursing myself for not wearing something more than a worn camisole and shorts to bed tonight. Fighting off an intruder with the bottom of my curvy ass hanging out isn't appealing. And the chill in the air turned my nipples to hard points as soon as I threw the covers back. The last thing I need is for some random, disgusting pervert to mistake that for interest.

I'm sure whichever lawyer is assigned to defend him would have a field day with that in court.

*Dios.* It's a sad day when you find yourself hoping whoever is trying to break into your room is a random pervert like any of the fifty who live in this building. But any one of them is better than the alternative. I stand a chance with them.

If Diego pushed one of his associates too far and they found out about me, I'm already dead. The long lost *principessa* whose father murdered the *Capo dei capi's* mother? Well, there's a reason I haven't been her since I was ten years old. Alvise and Diego knew exactly what would happen to me if anyone ever found out who I really am.

I hide behind the door, lifting the bat like I'm Roberto Clemente standing at home plate. I keep my body angled, and my feet planted like Diego taught me. My heart beats so loudly, I'm a little afraid it's going to give away my position. I hold my breath as the door creaks open.

A long shadow stretches across the floor, sinister in the darkness.

Bile crawls up my throat.

*Stay calm, Amalia*, I tell myself. *You can panic later.*

Yes, later. When I'm not dead or worse on my own bedroom floor. God, I hate this city. If it weren't for Diego, I would have packed up my stuff and left it in the rearview a long time ago. Between the gangs, the mobsters, and the run-of-the-mill criminals, street life is the only life left in entire sections of Chicago. At least it is in the sections I call home.

The shadow steps into the bedroom, the unmistak-able form of a man becoming apparent. He's tall and broad through the shoulders. It might be my imagina-

4

tion, but he looks like he's hunched over. Is he hiding something? I can't tell with the door partially blocking my view.

*It's probably his murder kit, Amalia. Gloves, rope, weapons. He came to hurt you. Kill you.*

He takes another step into the room.

I hold my breath, waiting for him to notice that I'm not in my bed.

Another step.

"Shit," he whispers, pausing.

Crap, he knows.

I act on instinct.

*"¡Vete al demonio!"* I yell, leaping out of my hiding spot and swinging the bat as hard as I can.

It slams into the side of the door with enough force to send a recoil up my arms. Wood splinters, pieces of the Masonite door caving in. The bat falls from my numb hands, landing on the carpet at my feet.

The man grabs me around the waist before I can dart out of the way.

Fight or flight kicks in, my heart pounding as adrenaline courses through me. I elbow him in the ribs. Hard. And then kick him in the shin.

"Jesus Christ, Lia," he grunts in pain. "What the fuck?"

"Diego?" My entire body goes lax as an over-whelming sense of relief courses through me, perme-ating every cell. I nearly crumple to the floor. And then indignation sets in. I rip myself out of his arms, mad as hell. "Are you insane? I thought you were a murderer!"

I stomp toward the door.

"I could have killed you!" I yell, slapping the switch so light floods into the room.

"You'd actually have to know how to aim your swing to do that," he says from behind me, pain and amusement mingling in his voice. And then I hear a thud.

I spin around, blinking twice to adjust to the light. When I do, it takes my mind a minute to catch up. My older brother is on his hands and knees on the floor, his dark head bent as if it's too heavy to hold up. He lists side to side, swaying like a toy boat on the lake.

"I didn't hit you that..." I trail off with a strangled cry when I catch sight of him. Anger retreats as cold fear sweeps in to take its place. Dried blood mats his dark hair, plastering it to his forehead on the right side. His right eye is swollen shut, his cheek one big bruise. More dried blood dots his lip.

The last time he looked this bad, I was in the seventh grade. Jorge Gutierrez called me an ugly cow. When I finally told Diego what he said, he stormed out of the house. He came home two hours later looking like death warmed over. Jorge and his friends looked even worse at school the next day. They never bothered me again either.

"Diego, what happened?" I whisper, dropping to my knees beside him.

"I'm in trouble, Lia," he says. "Big trouble this time." Diego isn't afraid of anything...but he's afraid now. For the first time ever, his voice shakes with it. So does his hand when he lifts it from the floor, reaching for mine.

"What do you mean? What did you do?" I ask, gripping his hand tightly in mine.

He lifts his head, one eye swollen shut. The other focuses on me through a haze of pain. The grim acceptance burning there sets my teeth on edge. "He knows what I've been doing. He's coming for me, Lia."

I don't have to ask who. I already know.

My blood runs cold.

## CHAPTER 1

# Rafe

"You're sure this is where he's hiding?" I ask my younger brother, Luca, flicking my gaze up and down the ancient apartment complex through the bulletproof window of the Bentayga. The rust-stained building looks more like a death trap than a habitable dwelling. Windows are boarded up in places, with graffiti declaring it gang territory. I assume the walls were tan at one point, though it wasn't any time in recent memory.

The parking lot is pitted and cracked, with entire sections of cement buckling. Brown patches of dead grass are scattered at random intervals throughout the yard. The swing-set off to the side of the building is broken, the chains long since rusted. The only piece of equipment on the small playground still in working order is the metal slide. Even that has large dents in it and a missing rung on the ladder. The picnic tables are broken.

How do people live like this? It's a far cry from Diego's luxury penthouse on The Loop. If he's hiding out here, he's gone as far underground in Chicago as he can go without vanishing from the city entirely. As if there's a rock big enough to hide him from my reach.

*Pezzo di merda.* Piece of shit. He's been dropping bodies all over Tommaso Genovese's territory and leaving a trail that leads right back to my doorstep.

"No," Luca says from the shadows beside me.

"Then why are we here?" I flick my stony gaze from the building to my brother.

He reclines against the seatback, hands loose at his sides, dark eyes focused out the window. He looks perfectly at ease, but I know better. Thanks to Diego Butera, my younger brother is a powder keg ready to blow.

He's not the only one, though I keep a tight leash on my anger, appearing as cold and emotionless as ever. I'm not. Inside, I'm seething with fury. Thanks to the machinations of our fucking lawyer, we may be tottering on the edge of war with the Genovese family. And we're currently so deep in the Latin Kings' territory, I'd be surprised if every gangbanger in Humboldt doesn't know we're here by now.

I haven't set foot in enemy territory in a decade. The Kings are no match for my family—no one is anymore. But I didn't get this far being foolish. I may have let my father shackle me to his fucking empire to spare my twin brother, Nico, a life in chains, but I have no intention of letting it kill me.

It's been two decades since Nico last spoke to me of his own free will. But he's alive and he's free. Luca and Gabriel, our youngest brother, are alive too. I haven't kept us safe this long just to die in a fucking drive-by. It'll take more than a gangbanger with a pistol and a pipe dream to take down the Valentino family.

No. If war comes, it'll be because *I* brought it. It won't be because I stepped foot in gang territory. And it certainly won't be because Diego decided to set us up to take the fall for his crimes with the Genovese family. People like the Latin Kings and the Genovese family may think they run the streets, but that's only because I let them. Everyone knows I rule this city.

Chicago is my sandbox, my kingdom. In a city where crime doesn't sleep, I'm a waking fucking nightmare. Nothing happens here without my approval.

*Except Diego Butera*, a little voice whispers.

The headache pounding behind my eyes ratchets up a notch. Not for the first time, I question how the hell we managed to miss what he was doing. As our lawyer, we trusted him more than most, and he betrayed us. How did Luca miss it? How did I? Better question, what does he stand to gain from sparking a war between us and the Genovese family?

I'm not sure I even want to know the answer to that question, but I intend to find out anyway. Unless I do, he may succeed, sparking a war guaranteed to be vicious and bloody. I've spent far too goddamn much of my life trying to avoid that very thing to let a motherfucker like Diego drag my family into one now.

"Butera stops by here twice a month," Luca says, his dark eyes still trained on the building across the street. "He stays for a few hours."

"He has someone here," I say, understanding dawning.

Luca nods, not looking at me.

"A girlfriend?"

"He's been coming for two years. Every Friday night."

*"Figlio di puttana,"* I mutter beneath my breath. *Son of a whore.* It is a woman.

Luca nods again, confirming what I already knew. He doesn't look at me, letting me decide for myself what I want to do with this information.

My soul is black with the sins I've committed to keep our father's empire in one piece but targeting women and children has never been among them. Some crimes, even I won't commit. The mass of scars on my abdomen burn as if to remind me why. I fight the urge to touch them, refusing to show that weakness to anyone, even my younger brother.

I trust him with my life. But Luca and Gabe weren't there the day our mother was gunned down and I was shot outside of an ice cream parlor. Once upon a time, Nico and I shared that burden between us. Now, I shoulder it alone. Somewhere on the far side of the city, Nico does the same. We're strangers now, our weaknesses our own.

As far as my twin is concerned, I'm as bad as the man who raised us. I'm the devil, the monster other monsters fear. He's not wrong...not entirely. But he's not right either. Not entirely. Not yet, anyway. Was the devil's soul gone before he slipped into hell, or did it die when the gates slammed closed behind him?

I have a feeling I'm going to live long enough to find out.

I flick my gaze to the window again, drumming my fingers against the leather seat as I try to decide what to do about the woman inside the apartment. Using her doesn't appeal to me on any level. Sooner or later, Diego will reappear. Rats always do. But I don't have time to wait for this one to crawl out of the gutter. If Tommaso Genovese gets his hands on Diego before I do, war may come whether I like it or not. Diego knows far too much about my family. I can't risk him striking a deal with Genovese.

But I've kept women out of it for twenty years, made them untouchable. Under my rule, our women are off-limits. If I change that rule now, I'm no better than my father.

*And if you don't, you're worse,* a little voice whispers. It's not wrong. My responsibility is to my brothers and my men, not to this woman. If dragging her into Diego's problems halts a war...there is no choice, is there?

*Pesante è la testa che indossa la corona.* Heavy is the head that wears the crown.

Fuck, I hate this job and all the bullshit that comes with it.

Raised voices capture my attention before I can

hammer the final nail in my coffin. I scan the front of the building, but don't see anything out of the ordinary. They're coming from inside. Judging from the sounds of it, the men I sent in to scout out the place found Diego's woman and she's less than thrilled about it. The argument rises in volume, punctuated by the crash of furniture and the shattering of glass.

A woman's voice cries out.

"What the fuck?" I growl, already reaching for the door handle as cold anger seizes me.

"Mattia," Luca says, his voice soft.

Next to my brothers, Mattia Agostino, my consigliere and closest friend, is the person I trust most in this world. Diego's girl could shiv Mattia between the ribs and he wouldn't lift a finger to stop her. I'm not the only one who knows what it's like to watch this way of life claim the life of a woman who didn't have a choice. Mattia's mother and father were murdered when we were seven.

I realize halfway out of the SUV that Luca isn't trying to warn me that Mattia is hurting the woman. He's telling me that Mattia is on the way out. My oldest friend ducks out of the apartment building behind a raven-haired Latina beauty. She's average height, her dark hair falling in waves midway down her back. It shines like silk in the afternoon sunlight. Even from a distance, the sway of her wide hips in her long skirt and the fire in her mocha eyes harden my cock.

A fist clenches around my heart, another around my balls. Both squeeze tight. And then tighter. What the fuck? I straighten to my full height, my gaze prowling across her. Whoever she is, Diego is a fucking idiot for hiding her here. She doesn't belong in this shit-hole. Cosa Nostra may have rules about women now, but the gangs of Chicago don't. They're honorless. This queen should be tucked up in a castle, surrounded by guards.

Christ, she's beautiful.

Her olive skin and luscious curves send beads of sweat trickling down my back.

"You," she growls, stomping toward me.

Mattia meets my gaze over her head, arching one brow as if to say *good luck with this one*.

I shift positions, restless in a way I've never been before. I plant my feet, forcing myself to stay still and let her come to me when my body actually vibrates with the desire to go to her. I shove my hands into my pockets, shaken for the first time in my life. I've done things that would horrify this girl, but *she's* what rattles me, what throws me off balance.

"Get your men out of my apartment," she says, her eyes flashing deadly fire when she draws to a stop in front of me. She barely comes up to my shoulder, allowing me to see right down her modest little blouse. She seems to know who I am, but she doesn't flinch or show fear. She tips her chin back, meeting my gaze boldly. "Diego isn't hiding in my underwear drawer."

I glance from her to Mattia in silent question.

"She threw a lamp at Vito's head when he got close to the dresser," he says, shrugging one meaty shoulder. "I told him to check it out."

"I should have thrown a second lamp," she says, a

certain savage satisfaction in her tone. Her fearlessness does a number on my cock. She can't be older than twenty-one or twenty-two, but she doesn't waver. Men three times her age quiver in fear when they face me. Not this woman. Who is she?

*Mine.*

Yes, I like the sound of that. This fierce little tigress is mine. Diego can't argue from the grave. He's not worthy of her anyway. If he were, he wouldn't have her hidden away like a dirty secret. She'd be tucked up in his penthouse on The Loop, living in luxury the way she deserves instead of in squalor here.

Why the fuck is he hiding her here?

"What's your name, *tigrotta*?"

"My name is irrelevant," she says, brushing off my question. "You came here looking for Diego. He isn't here. You and your men can leave now."

"Her name is Amalia Santiago."

She turns a venomous scowl on Mattia.

"Amalia," I say, unable to resist. It's a beautiful name. I can't wait to whisper it in the dark when I'm fucking my kid into her. I'll say it again and again, until she hears it in her dreams. "Where is your boyfriend, *tigrotta*?"

"Of course that's what you assume," she says, rolling her eyes at me.

"He's not her boyfriend," Mattia says, translating her annoyance. He's far better at understanding women than I am. Save for my housekeeper, there hasn't been a woman in my life since I was a teenager. People say it's because I'm a heartless bastard. Their whispers suit my purposes, so I let them think it. But the truth is I never let myself get close enough to one to risk falling. I may have made my world safer for women, but that doesn't mean one deserves to be shackled to a motherfucker like me. "I believe they grew up together."

Interesting. Diego's father, Alvise Butera, was one of my father's associates. He was never fully one of us, but he was never entirely on the outside, either. Diego grew up in our territory. This girl didn't. I'd remember her. You don't forget perfection like this.

"I don't know where he is," Amalia says, casting another dark glower at Mattia before turning back to me. I'm sure she intends it to be fierce, but it's just fucking cute if you ask me. She's a kitten facing down a lion. Her claws are sharp, but they're soft. "He doesn't tell me where he goes or what he does. Even if he did, I wouldn't tell you. I know who you are."

"Then you know why I'm here," I say, my voice soft.

A shadow passes through her mocha eyes, letting me know I'm right. She knows, if not everything, then enough to know this visit doesn't end with Diego living a long, happy life. And yet he left her here anyway. Either he's confident I won't involve her...or she means less to him than Luca thinks. I'm not prepared to say it's the latter. Not if they've known each other since they were kids. Not if he's been coming here twice a month like clockwork. Not if she knows he's in deep. She means something to him. He's just banking on the fact that I won't hurt her because she's female.

The arrogant bastard thinks I'll dance on his strings, bound by my own honor. If Amalia were anyone else, he'd be right. I'd let her go simply because I'm *not* my father. Luca, Gabe...every man on my payroll chose this life, same as I did. We knew the risks. We accepted them anyway.

If war comes, we die bloody. It is what it is.

But Diego seriously fucking misjudged the content of my character. I may not be my father, but I'm still the motherfucker this city loses sleep worrying about. And I want this girl beneath me, her nails embedded in my skin. When it comes to some things, there is no honor. There's only want. And take.

I want. And I'm taking.

No, that's not right. I *need*. It's damn near a compulsion at this point. She's mine.

I'll burn this entire fucking complex to the ground before I leave here without this girl.

"You're lying," I say, taking a step toward her. She doesn't back up. She doesn't waver. My dick throbs in the face of her defiance. Will she be as fearless in bed? As fiery? "I think you do know where he is, Amalia. But I think you'd rather sell your soul than tell me."

*"No hago tratos con el diablo." I don't make deals with the devil.* She flings the insult at me in Spanish, but I speak the language fluently.

"You'll make a deal with this devil, *tesoro*," I say, taking another step toward her. The toes of my dress shoes land flush against her ballet flats. Her cinnamon and vanilla scent swirls around me. I grit my teeth, fighting the urge to snarl like an unruly beast. I press closer, until her tits graze my chest.

*Ah, tesoro. Your ripe little body tells a story your eyes would deny.*

She knows I feel those hard little nipples. She grits her teeth, her cheeks flushing. Her defiant gaze never wavers from mine.

"Tell me where he is, or I'm taking you in his place," I whisper, already knowing she isn't going to tell me where Diego is...already knowing I'm not really giving her a choice at all. As we've already established, there aren't any lines I won't cross if it gets me what I want. *Her.*

"Go to hell," she whispers.

I hold her gaze for a long, silent moment before lifting my head. "Mattia, pack her things," I say. "She's coming home with me."

"I'll scream."

"Do it then," I say, one corner of my lip lifting in an amused smile. "Scream." I step closer, pressing our bodies together in one long line. The top of her head fits perfectly beneath my chin. I tilt my head, putting my mouth next to her ear. "See how much blood I'll spill to keep you, Amalia."

She gasps quietly.

*"Eres mío ahora." You're mine now.* I say it in Spanish instead of Italian to make sure she understands.

"Your prisoner," she spits, pushing away from me with her hands on my chest. Flames scorch me when her eyes meet mine. "Fine. I'll go with you. But hell will freeze over before I tell you anything about Diego."

She means it, and I have no intentions of making her eat her words. As soon as he finds out I have her, he'll come looking for her. He'll tell me everything I want to know by himself. If he thinks he's taking her from me though, he's sadly mistaken.

Amalia Santiago may think I'm the devil...but she's about to become my queen.

## CHAPTER 2

*Amalia*

My whole life, I've heard stories of Rafael, Luca, and Gabriel Valentino. It's impossible to live in this city and not hear whispers of the three wicked brothers who rule it from the shadows...or of the fourth brother, the twin who walked away long ago. One twin, Rafael, is a mob boss. The other, Nico, is an astrophysicist, a professor at Northwestern. I've never met any of them, yet their lives intersect mine in ways none of us can undo.

Because of my father, they lost their mother. Because of theirs, I grew up an orphan. Rafael doesn't know this, of course. No one except Diego knows. It's fitting, I suppose, that he's the reason I'm now Rafael's prisoner when I'm part of the reason Diego is in this mess to begin with. His vendetta against the Valentino family began when his real father disappeared when he was fifteen. It only grew when he and Alvise Butera found me in a group home a few years later.

I don't blame Rafael for what his father did to

mine. I'm not even sure I blame his father. My father fired the first bullet in that war. He murdered an innocent woman in cold blood. It's hard to grieve for someone capable of doing that. It's hard to grieve for someone I don't even remember. I was only two when he and my mom died.

The system swallowed me up, stripping me of any memories I had. By the time Alvise found me eight years later, I knew nothing but my name. Not everyone had forgotten the long lost *principessa* though. Lorenzo Valentino hadn't forgotten. Neither had Alvise. He took me in, protected me so Lorenzo would never find me. Everything I knew vanished overnight. He changed my name, taught me Spanish, hid me away in gang territory.

Diego blames the Valentinos for stripping me of my identity and my birthright. He *hates* them for it. He won't rest until their empire is in ashes. And I've let him drag me into the middle of his crusade.

To save his life, I'm not sure I have another choice.

He's the only family I have left since Alvise died.

But I think I've officially lost my mind. Because I just let Rafael Valentino take me prisoner.

I glare at him across the SUV, wishing my elderly Haitian neighbor had taught me some of the Hoodoo she swears by. I wouldn't mind speaking a few curses into existence right about now. I've never seen any of the Valentino brothers in person until now. Rafael's picture has been splashed across every news station and magazine in the city, but nothing prepared me for the reality of meeting him. I thought I'd be afraid...I'm not.

I thought he'd look like a criminal...he doesn't. He's a dark prince. And an overgrown bully.

There's something arresting about him. A fire burning deep in the pits of his chocolate eyes. Everything about him is still. Cold. Austere. He's every inch the king, imposing and steely. From the top of his dark head to the tips of his shiny shoes, he's dark—black hair, black eyes, olive skin, black suit, crisp white button down beneath. I don't think there's darkness in him. I think he was *made* from darkness.

But the fire burning in his eyes makes me want to creep a little bit closer. There's something there, some emotion that doesn't make sense to me. It's...soft. But what does a man like him know about softness?

*Nothing, Amalia,* I tell myself. *And don't you dare forget it. Stick to the plan.*

The plan. Right.

If I make it out of this alive, I'm killing Diego. We should have run when we had the chance. There's no way I'm going to get close enough to Rafael to get my hands on the information Diego wants. As soon as I get anywhere close to his office, he's going to kill me and hide my body where no one will ever find it. There will be no proving any of the Valentinos' crimes.

Just like there was never any proving their father had my parents killed. Lawyers like Diego aren't the only reason charges don't stick to men like Rafael. There is no justice when those meant to mete it out are just as guilty as those on trial. God works hard, but no one works harder than a pillar of society with a penchant for bad behavior and a reputation to protect.

They hand out favors like lollipops to keep their misdeeds hidden.

"If you think Diego is going to come for me, you're wrong," I tell Rafael.

"We'll see."

"You'll see," I say. "I already know he isn't coming. We aren't that close." We are that close, but I made him swear not to come, no matter what. If he does, Rafael will kill him, and then all of this will have been for nothing.

"And yet you're here now. You're putting yourself through a lot of trouble for someone you *aren't that close* with, *tesoro*."

"It was your charming personality," I say, rolling my eyes. My stomach threatens to flutter at the term of endearment rolling from his lips. It's far more sensual than it should be. I like it far more than I should. "I just couldn't resist spending days on end being held captive by you. It seemed like such a good use of my time."

"She's going to be a problem," the man beside Rafael says suddenly. It's the first time he's spoken since Rafael escorted me to the fancy SUV ten minutes ago.

I shift my gaze from Rafael to him. He's sitting in the shadows, almost like he's trying to hide in them. Like Rafael, he's a wickedly handsome dark prince— olive skin, black hair, and chocolate eyes. He's familiar too, though I've never seen him before either. I think he's one of the younger brothers, but I'm not sure which one. Luca? Gabe? I don't know.

Even after Lorenzo and Alvise died, the hiding never really ended. Diego always worried Rafael would find out about me and come for me, just like Alvise always worried Lorenzo would.

He was right. Rafael did come. Only...we *wanted* him to come.

And I'm wildly out of my depth. I know nothing about his world. Nothing about the people in it. Aside from the whispers that reach me, these men are strangers to me, complete unknowns. Diego rarely spoke of them after Alvise died, refusing to let this part of his life touch me.

The other man's lips quirk into an amused smirk when he sees me glaring at him.

It looks natural on him, which surprises me. When Rafael smiled, it looked sinister and unused, as if it's not something he does often. I don't get the same impression from this man. He seems less...rigid, but no less intense.

"I know she is," Rafael says.

"*She* has a name," I say, my voice saccharine. "And she is going to be a huge problem." I give them a blinding smile, showing my teeth. I hope Rafael takes it for the warning it is. I may have let him take me, but I'm not a complete idiot. I don't trust him. I'm not safe with him. I don't believe for one minute that Rafael won't slit my throat while I sleep if he finds out that we planned for him to take me.

My only chance here is to fight him at every available opportunity. I have to make him believe I don't want to be here...which shouldn't be hard since I don't actually want to be here. Lying might not come easy, but being a brat? Well, if he wants to call me a little tiger, I'll show him my claws. God knows, something about him makes me want to show them. Every time he looks at me, I want to misbehave just to throw his neat little world into chaos.

I don't know what that's about and I don't want to know.

"Jesus Christ," the other man says, and then exhales a sharp laugh, looking from me to his brother. "Rather you than me, brother."

"Fuck off, Luca."

"You're Luca?" I turn curious eyes on him, expecting him to look...different now that I know who he is, but he doesn't. He's second in command in the Valentino family, nearly as powerful as his brother. Yet darkness doesn't cling to him the way it does to Rafael. His amused grin still seems easy, as if he wears one often.

"Diego told you my name," he says.

"This city told me your name," I correct with a shake of my head. "It might be hard to hear the whispers from up in your ivory tower, but they're quite loud down here with the common folk."

"Are they?" His lips twitch.

"Mmhmm."

"What do the rumors say, *tesoro*?" Rafael asks.

"About Luca?" I meet his gaze. "Much less than they do about you."

"What do they say about me?"

"Mostly that you're a murderous fiend who gets off on terrorizing people."

"Jesus," Luca says with another laugh.

I fight the urge to squirm. I shouldn't have said that. It is what people say though. They've been saying it for years. Anytime anyone disappears in this city, they blame Rafael. When someone dies under suspicious circumstances, it doesn't take long before people start whispering that Rafael had them killed for one reason or another.

People call him the devil because they fear him. He's the bogeyman, the monster that grows more monstrous with each retelling. Who knows how much is truth and how much is fiction at this point? But it's not all fiction, that much is certain. This man has blood on his hands, and a lot of it. He isn't a good man. And yet...and yet something about him attracts me anyway.

*Absolutely not, Amalia. No. No way.*

"Do you believe them?"

I turn to stare out the window instead of answering, not sure he'd like the answer if I gave it. The city passes in silent blurs as we leave gang territory behind... as we leave *my* territory behind. No one is ever safe where I live, but I'm far safer there than where we're going.

My soul is, anyway. The devil can't claim it there.

"Answer me, Amalia," Rafael demands, his voice soft.

I turn my gaze back to him to find his dark eyes locked on me, that same fire burning in them. It lights up something inside me, sets it to burning too. Do I believe the rumors? Hell yes, I do. Only an idiot looks at a lion and believes he's a lamb.

"Is there a reason I shouldn't?" I ask, cocking a brow.

"Not every rumor is true," he says.

"But most have a little truth to them."

He sighs, but he doesn't disagree.

We both know he can't.

Half an hour later, we stop at a massive gate so security can buzz us through. Perfectly pruned bushes line the driveway on both sides, sculpted into impressive shapes. I catch glimpses of rolling green grass and fountains beyond. And then the house itself comes into view. My rundown apartment complex could easily fit within.

Imposing columns shoot into the air, standing like sentinels on either side of the massive front doors. Ivy climbs up the stone walls, lending an air of antiquity to it.

This place isn't a home. It's a fortress, every bit the ivory tower I called it earlier. Only it's brick instead of white... and somehow made more overwhelming because of it.

A dozen men in black suits line the circular driveway, each standing in the exact same position. Each wearing the exact same expression. They're replicas of one another, all twelve of them big, muscular, overwhelmingly large.

The SUV rolls to a stop in front of the steps.

My stomach trembles for the first time since I marched outside to confront Rafael. I fight the urge to fidget, schooling my features into a mask of cool disdain. Inside, I'm a mess of nerves, swallowing back the bile creeping up my throat.

One of the men steps forward to open the door of the SUV.

Rafael casts a glance at me that's a quagmire of dark and light. It confuses me, makes me ache in ways and places that shouldn't be possible. He slides out without saying anything, his leather and brandy scent wreaking havoc on my already overloaded system. He murmurs something to his man and then reaches back for my hand.

"Come, *tesoro*," he says, his voice as soft as ever.

I don't think he has to raise it to be heard and obeyed. People probably jump to keep him happy. Part of me wants to defy him just to see what he'll do. Just to unravel him and that control he wears like armor. I *want* to know what he's like underneath it, what secrets he hides beneath that insufferable mask of cool command and cold indifference. But I don't think this is the time to satisfy my curiosity.

I take his hand instead, letting him help me from the SUV. His hand is warm around mine, sending a frisson of heat up my arm. He keeps me pressed to his side, almost as if to protect me from these men.

Why?

"This is Amalia," he says, a razor-sharp edge to his voice that catches me off guard. This is the Rafael that holds this city in an iron grip, the one they fear. This is their king speaking. "If a single hair on her head is harmed, you'll die by my hand. Interfere between us, and you'll answer to me. Treat her with anything less than respect, you'll wish for death. Touch her, and I'll kill you so slowly you'll *beg* for death."

A shiver works its way through me. He means every word.

"Yes, sir," eleven voices say at once. The twelfth mouths the words, but I don't think he actually speaks them. His eyes are locked on me, something...malevolent in them. He's maybe twenty-five, with a scar across his temple and a wildness about him. There's something familiar about him, but I can't place what. Whoever he is, he's dangerous. I feel that truth bubbling in my stomach.

I instinctively take a step closer to Rafael, cowering into him. He lets go of my hand to wrap his around my hip. His frosty gaze skims over his men, his intent clear. He's declaring ownership, stamping me with his seal of possession. He isn't trying to protect me. He wants them to think I *belong* to him.

I bristle silently, swallowing back the urge to tell him here and now that I belong to no man. I don't. I never have. When you're curvy like me, men look right through you. Or, worse, they see you and mock you. They don't jump to date you. They certainly don't claim you because they want you. Whatever game he's playing, it has nothing to do with me.

His men are still watching us, the dangerous one smiling like he finds something amusing about this whole situation. So I lean into Rafael instead, playing his little game with him. If he's surprised, he doesn't show it. He simply squeezes my hip and then turns his face slightly so his lips brush my crown.

*"Bienvenida a casa, mi reinita."*

*Welcome home, my little queen.*

The gates of hell creak open.

"Come," he says a moment later. "Luca, wait here."

Luca's soft laugh floating from the SUV is the only response he gets, and then he's leading me up the steps. Two men fall into step behind us.

"*Tesoro*, this is Coda and Domani. They'll be your guards," Rafael says.

"You pronounced jailers wrong," I say as sweetly as possible.

He cuts his eyes in my direction. "No. I said guards correctly, *tigrotta*."

I snort.

"They'll protect you with their lives."

"From you?"

"You don't need protection from me."

I snort again, and then stop walking to glance

around. His house is beautiful, but cold. Like a mausoleum. There's no warmth here, no life. Everything is neatly arranged, not a speck of dust in sight, not a single item out of place. The porcelain floors shine. Expensive furniture gleams with polish. There are no family photos on the walls, no trinkets on the tables. Everything is just...cold.

"You grew up here?" I ask.

"Yes." He leads me to the stairs, his guards following behind us.

"How old were you when your mom was murdered?"

"How do you know she was murdered?"

*Because my father killed her.*

"Everyone knows," I lie, not stupid enough to spill that secret.

"Eleven."

My heart pulses with sympathy. No wonder he is the way he is. He was just a little boy, forced to grow up in a place like this. I've been here less than five minutes, and the chill is already seeping its way into my soul. He's been here for decades.

*Don't you dare feel sorry for him, Amalia*, I snap to myself. *Don't soften. He'll eat you alive.*

"I'm not your possession," I say, forcing myself to focus on that. "And this isn't my home."

"It is now, *tigrotta*."

"I'm out of here as soon as I find a way," I warn him.

He gives me another smile, though it doesn't reflect in his eyes. Nothing but the devil lurks there, as if he's daring me to try it. Why do I get the impression that he *wants* me to try to run? "Try it, *tesoro*. You won't make it through the fucking door before I drag you back."

I briefly contemplate pushing him down the stairs, if for no other reason than watching him bounce down them would bring me immense satisfaction. But the thought only lasts a second before I discard it. Unlike him, I'm not a violent person. I don't hurt people, not even those with hellfire burning where their souls are supposed to be. Besides, pushing him down the stairs isn't going to get me any closer to my goal. If anything, it'll just seal my fate that much quicker.

Instead of saying anything, I elbow him in the ribs and then storm up the stairs. He laughs quietly behind me. Within two steps, he's at my side again, his hand on my elbow. He guides me down the hall to the left, and then down another hallway to the right. We twist and turn down hallways each more lavishly appointed than the last. And yet none of them are homey or warm in any way.

"How many ghosts haunt this place?" I mutter, only partially kidding.

"Too many," he says, steering me toward the end of the hall.

"Coda and Domani aren't coming?" I peer over my shoulder. They're at the end of the hall, their backs to us.

"They don't enter my personal quarters."

That draws me up short.

"Your personal quarters?" I gape at him. "I am *not* sharing a room with you."

His smile reflects in his eyes this time. The bastard. It overtakes his features, turning him from dark prince to wicked, wanton king. Those chocolate eyes rake like fire across me, kicking up flames deep in my stomach. "Oh, you're definitely sleeping in my bed, *tigrotta*," he says. "It's the only fucking way I'll get any sleep with you under this roof."

"I am not sleeping with you," I hiss, yanking my elbow out of his hold. Hell will freeze over before I sleep with him. Matter of fact, I think hell might switch polarities entirely before that happens. I don't care how dangerous he is or how badly Diego needs my help or how much my stomach quivers at the thought of sharing a bed with this man. It's not happening.

He ignores me, instead stepping around me to open the door. He enters the room, still without saying anything. I stand there for several long moments, my feet rooted in place, waiting for him to come back out so we can finish this argument. He doesn't.

"You have got to be kidding me," I growl, stomping after him.

I barely make it over the threshold before I'm pressed up against the wall, his knee wedged between my thighs, his body pinning mine in place. His mouth comes down on mine in a hard kiss. I try to resist him. I *want* to resist him. But as soon as his tongue touches mine, my resolve weakens. I unravel, losing touch with reality as a surge of desire swarms through me so fast, I cry out in shock...in bliss.

Rafael growls, plunging one hand into the thick mass of my hair. He cranes my head back, angling it to allow himself to kiss me deeper. He's not cold now. Oh no. He's a livewire, sparking against me again and again as he consumes my mouth with his wicked lips and honeyed tongue. His control slips, his teeth raking across my bottom lip.

"Fight me, *tigrotta*," he growls against my lips. "Sink your little claws into me and fight like hell if it makes you happy. But you will be sleeping in my bed. It'll be my cock you dream about. And when you can't stand the ache between your thighs anymore, I'll be the one you reach for. It'll be my cock fucking you so deep you'll feel me every time you breathe. You're *mine*, Amalia."

"I'm not a possession," I gasp, writhing as he grinds his knee against my center.

"No," he whispers, trailing kisses across my cheek. His lips dance down the side of my throat. His stubble scratches my skin, sending a bolt of lava through my veins. "You could never be something as simple as that, *tesoro*. You're going to be my queen."

Before I can react to that, he's gone.

I slide down the wall, my legs too weak to hold me up. My mind reeling.

The door clicks closed behind him.

A second later, the lock slides into place.

The arrogant bastard locked me in.

"I'm going to kill you, Diego," I whisper, my entire body trembling, though I'm not sure if I'm trembling with fear...or with need.

"**D**id you find anything in her belongings?" I ask Mattia, glancing up at him when he steps inside my office two hours later. Luca is gone, off to fill Gabe in on the situation. With any luck, Diego will know within a matter of days that Amalia is here. All I have to do is wait for the motherfucker to show up. Sooner or later, he will. And then we can end this whole shitshow.

Amalia is a completely different situation. If I want her to fall in love with me, I need her to trust me. But it's already a little too late for that. Holding her here against her will isn't going to win me any favors. I doubt kissing her won me any either. I don't regret it though. Every time she opens that smart mouth, I want to fuck the fight out of her. Her fire is a hell of a turn on. She's not a delicate flower, or a trembling little leaf. She's a queen, a woman worthy of a throne. She deserves better than a soulless bastard like me, but I'm claiming her anyway.

If anyone would like to try to stop me, well, they won't be the first murder I've committed. Probably won't be the last either. At least this one will have a reason beyond this goddamn empire. My father might be burning in hell, but he's doing it with a smile on his face, I'm sure.

Under my rule, his empire is secure. We're the strongest of all the families. For the first time in nearly one hundred years, a *Capo dei capi* reigns. Me.

Mattia closes the door behind him. "She doesn't belong there," he says, strolling across the office toward me. "Her things are too new, too nice. High end. He's trying to hide her where no one would think to look."

Gang territory is certainly the place to do it. We don't fuck around in the area I've given to them. In exchange, they keep their little wars out of my territory. The gang leaders may chafe under my rule, but they aren't foolish enough to try to challenge me. If they were, I wouldn't have made it out of LK territory without a confrontation today.

Instead, they let me walk in and take her without objection. They're too busy with their own beefs to even think about trying to take me on. Even if they did, they wouldn't survive. They're children, trying to play with giants. We perfected the game long ago and they know it.

"Diego grew up in our territory," I muse, sliding the brandy decanter across the desk toward Mattia. "She didn't."

"Diego moved out of our territory when Alvise retired," Mattia says, pouring himself a finger of brandy.

"Could have met her then. You know Alvise had a thing for bringing home strays."

My brows pull together at the thought of Amalia as a stray. I don't like it, the possibility of her growing up with no family, no home. Even a place like this and a father like mine is better than a life like that, especially for an innocent little girl. If Alvise did take her in, he did her a favor.

"A better question is why has Diego been hiding her for so long?" Mattia points his glass at me and then quickly swallows the amber liquid. "Because he's been with us for years, but none of us knew about this girl until Luca started digging."

"Either he had a plan all along or he didn't want us finding out about her," I agree, already having worked that out for myself. How long has he been hiding her in gang territory, moving her from place to place to keep her from being found?

"Or both."

"*Figlio di puttana*," I mutter, not sure which it is. Not sure what he's out to accomplish here or why. Was he simply worried about this exact outcome, or are we missing something? I don't know. And not knowing is pissing me off.

Being in the dark isn't a feeling I'm used to. I'm always two steps ahead, planning for moves my enemies haven't even thought about making yet. Diego's betrayal was something I didn't see coming. He has no motive, nothing to win here. At least not that we can see. It makes no fucking sense. He loses just as much as everyone else in this scenario.

A war between us and the Genovese family paints a target on his back too. He's our lawyer, for fuck's sake. He'll be one of the first on our payroll they try to squeeze. If he doesn't flip, they'll clip him. Either way, he ends up with a bullet between his eyes.

"Fuck," Mattia growls, dropping his glass on the desk abruptly. He yanks his earpiece from his ear and taps his watch. "Say that again."

"Uh, you might want to get up here," Coda says through the speaker on Mattia's watch. "The boss told us not to touch the girl, but she's currently escaping over the balcony."

Why am I not surprised? Christ, she's going to make me crazy before she gives an inch. And I'm going to let her do it. But not by putting herself in danger.

"How, exactly, is she escaping over the balcony?" I ask.

"Uh, boss," Coda says, clearly reluctant to be the bearer of bad news. "She used your clothes to make a rope and she's using it to climb down, sir."

"Jesus Christ." I jump to my feet, already headed for the door.

"I'll take upstairs," Mattia says, hot on my heels.

We split at the stairs. I jog out the front door, my heart in my throat. If she falls... My stomach churns at the thought. If she falls, it'll be my fault for locking her in and leaving her there. I've known her for a matter of hours, and I already know she isn't the type to cool her heels and wait to be summoned. Left to her own devices, she'll set this place on fire and then smile while it burns to ash around me.

A group of my men are gathered on the back lawn, milling restlessly beneath my balcony. A rope made from thousand-dollar leather belts and my pants dangles five feet from the ground, the legs tied together to reinforce them.

My heart stops when I see Amalia dangling in midair, nothing but the makeshift rope holding her aloft. She's already closer to the ground than the balcony, but still far too high up for comfort. Even from this angle, I can tell she's pale and trembling, gripping her makeshift rope with both hands.

"Boss," Ricci says, expelling a breath. "She won't listen to us."

Of course she won't. Stubborn, brilliant woman.

"Amalia."

"R-R-Rafael?" She has her eyes squeezed tightly closed.

"Yeah, *tesoro*. It's Rafe."

Is it my imagination or do her shoulders sag with relief?

"I messed up," she whispers. "I f-forgot I'm scared of heights."

*Ah, tesoro.*

"Listen to me, *tigrotta*. You're already halfway down. I just need you to climb a little lower, and then I'll catch you."

"You can't catch me!" she cries.

"Why not?"

"I'm not answering that in front of your men, Rafael Valentino," she huffs, switching from terrified kitten to bristling tiger again.

I frown, trying to work out why she doesn't want to answer me in front of my men, but come up with nothing. She let me touch her in front of them earlier. "I don't understand," I reluctantly say, chafing at the admission. Not knowing everything about her is intolerable.

"You can't catch me," she says, the words stiff.

"Amalia, climb down. I'll catch you," I promise, refusing to waste time arguing over this.

"No."

My men shift restlessly. No one tells me no. Ever.

What does it say about me that I like when this curvy little queen does it? My whole fucking life, people have been giving me exactly what I want, no questions asked. They jump to obey as if their lives depend on it. Not Amalia. She defies me as if it's her job. And god*damn*, I can't get enough. Her bravado. That fierce defiance. The way she looks at me as if I'm the biggest disappointment she's ever met in her life. Even now, she has my dick so hard, I want to drag her to the ground and fuck her raw.

"Now, *tesoro*," I growl instead, the thought of any of these motherfuckers seeing her lost in pleasure sending a ripple of jealousy through me. It's not rational. There's nothing sane about it. But I'd destroy every fucking one of them.

"Fine!" Amalia cries as Mattia appears on the balcony overhead. "But if I hurt you, it's your own fault! And I probably won't even be sorry!"

Hurt me? How she thinks that's possible is beyond me.

"Mattia, Ricci, support the rope," I order, filing that comment away to deal with when she isn't in imminent danger.

Once Mattia and Ricci have the rope secured to keep it from swinging, thus reducing the risk of it shaking her loose, she slowly begins to lower herself. Despite wanting to spank her gorgeous ass for putting herself in danger like this, I'm impressed by her ingenuity. Using pants and belts instead of sheets allowed her to create hand and footholds. Her rope is probably the most expensive rope in the entire state, but it's impressive.

"Just a few more feet, *tesoro*," I say, watching like a hawk as she descends toward me.

"Don't tell me!" she cries. "I don't want to know."

The tremor in her voice is the only thing that keeps me from laughing. She's legitimately afraid, perhaps for the first time today. I can't help but think she's only trying to get away this hard because I kissed her earlier. No, I didn't kiss her. I consumed her.

I should feel like a fucking asshole for forcing her to sleep in my bed when the idea clearly distresses her so much she's willing to endure this to get away from me. I *do* feel like an asshole. Guilt lashes at me, but I tamp it down, ruthlessly quelling it. Putting her in my bed isn't about getting in her pants. As much as I want to fuck my kid into her, putting her in my room is about protection, plain and simple.

My fight is with Diego Butera. I brought her here to draw him out, not to harm her. That makes her mine to protect. This world killed my mom while I stood by helplessly and watched, unable to protect her. I won't allow it to claim Amalia's life. If anyone thinks to come for her, they'll have to go through me to get to her.

Her hand slips, throwing her off balance. She scrambles for the handhold but can't get to it in time. She plummets backward toward the ground with a sharp cry of terror that I know I'll hear in my nightmares.

A ripple of worry goes through my men, every one of them rocking forward on their heels as if to catch her before they remember my vow to kill anyone who touches her. It wasn't an empty threat, and they know it. My father may have bound me to this fucking empire, but I blackened my soul all on my own. My hands are stained with blood I spilled, so much of it I lost count long ago.

I step forward, opening my arms while my men silently deliberate whether an emergency changes my threat. It doesn't. No one touches her. *No one.* Call me what you will, but I've had my hands on her gorgeous body. I know what kind of magic she works. One kiss, and I'm already tripping down the path to obsession. I won't allow anyone else to get close enough to think about trying to take her from me.

Amalia lands in my arms with a squeak, her momentum nearly dragging us both to the ground. I secure her against my chest, exhaling a ragged breath into her hair.

"Are you okay, *tesoro*?" I ask.

"You caught me."

"I'll always catch you."

She bursts into tears.

"Ah, *tesoro*," I sigh, holding her close to my heart. *My heart.* Since meeting her today, for the first time in a long time, I feel it beating. Pounding like a war drum against my rib cage. It might be my imagination, but I think it's beating her name.

My men step aside, allowing us through.

She cries quietly as I carry her inside. Instead of taking her back upstairs, I take her to the library. A neutral space. It was always my mother's favorite. When Nico and I were little boys, it was our favorite too. I stopped coming here after she died. Nico never did.

Perhaps that's why he retained so much of her light. It left me long ago, but it never left Nico. He's always been more like her than any of us. He used to spend hours in here, looking through his telescope at the stars, searching for heaven.

I've always wondered if he ever found it. I've never had the courage to ask. Even if it's real, I'm not headed there. Why torment myself with hope of a place I'll never see? If one of us gets to spend eternity with our mother, it won't be me.

I carry Amalia to the sofa and sit with her in my lap. She's not crying now, but she's stiff in my arms. Winning her trust is going to take a miracle, but I try anyway.

"I won't hurt you, *tesoro*," I say softly, rubbing my hand down her back. "Regardless of what Diego told you, I'm not the kind of man who abuses innocent women."

"You want to sl-sleep with me."

"I do," I say, not lying to her. I won't do that. "But I'm not going to take you against your will, Amalia. When you give yourself to me, it'll be because you want me too. It won't be by force. It won't be because you think you don't have a choice. It'll be because you ache for me."

"I..." She pulls back, her tear-stained face wary, and still so goddamn beautiful. "I'm sorry I ruined your clothes."

"Fuck my clothes," I growl, leaning in to brush tears from her cheeks. "Ruin whatever you want to ruin. I don't give a fuck. Fight me. Burn this house down around me. But don't put yourself in danger, *tesoro*. Not because you're pissed at me. Believe me, I'm not worth it."

Her mocha gaze slides across my face, searching for something. I'm not sure if she finds it, but a little furrow etches itself between her brows. "You're confusing me," she whispers.

"Yeah?"

She nods.

"Then that makes two of us. You've been confusing me all day, *tigrotta*."

Of course that makes her smile. Beautiful little *folletta*.

"I'll make you a deal, *tesoro*."

"I thought we covered this already. I don't make deals with the devil, Rafe."

"We did." I brush my thumb over her bottom lip, unable to resist. The urge to kiss her again beats at me, but I fight it off, unwilling to shatter the tentative, fragile threads of peace we've only just begun to forge. I need her trust. Perhaps more than I've ever needed anything. Not because of Diego. Not because I don't want her trying to sneak out as soon as my back is turned. But because I want her to believe in me enough to let her guard down. I want her to see *me*. "But you'll want to make this deal with the devil, Amalia."

She eyes me placidly, waiting to hear me out.

"If you'll agree not to endanger yourself trying to run away, I'll give you free run of the house. You can go anywhere except the west wing."

Her eyes narrow in suspicion. "Is there an enchanted rose and a magic mirror in the west wing?"

I feel my lips twitch. "You think I'm a beast."

"If the Disney movie fits," she says with a shrug.

"I have no enchanted furniture, Amalia."

"Why can't I go into the west wing?"

"Because I said so."

The furrow between her brows deepens, her expression growing frosty. "Try again."

Of course a simple order isn't good enough for her. She wasn't made to fall in line. She was made to question everything and never back down. Isn't that what's had my dick hard all day?

"The west wing is where my men who stay on the property reside," I say, willingly giving her what I'd give no one else. "I don't want you in their quarters."

"Oh." She purses her lips. "I can go anywhere else in the house?"

"You can even go outside so long as either myself, Mattia, Coda, or Domani are with you."

"Fine."

My sigh of relief is short-lived.

"Just so you know, you didn't say I couldn't run away. You just said I couldn't endanger myself trying," she says, smiling at me so brightly I know I just got played. She slides off my lap, her chin held high. "I hope you don't have much to do while I'm here because I plan to run away a lot."

*Mafankulo.*

Why does that make my dick so hard?

Do I even need to ask?

Everything about this girl makes my dick hard.

"Why didn't you want me to catch you?" I ask, determined to get to the bottom of that while we're clearing shit up.

She fidgets, glancing away from me. And then she huffs. "I didn't want to squish you, okay?"

"Squish me?" My brows furrow.

"Isn't your brother a scientist?"

I stare at her, not sure what her point is.

"Physics," she says, rolling her eyes. "Gravity, velocity, acceleration, kinematics? Does any of this ring a bell?"

"Nico is the scientist, *tesoro.*"

"Objects pick up speed when they fall, Rafe. I'm a big girl," she says, throwing up her hands. "I didn't want to hurt you."

What the fuck?

"What the fuck?" I growl, glaring at her. "You aren't fucking fat, Amalia. Who said that shit to you?"

"Um, basically everyone my whole life?" She rolls

her eyes again. "I know what I look like. I know what size I wear. I'm not ashamed of my body or who I am. I don't care what anyone else thinks or what they have to say about me. But the fact remains that I was worried I'd hurt you if I fell on your stupid head. Clearly, that didn't happen. So it doesn't even matter."

"I want names, *tesoro*," I growl, climbing to my feet and pacing toward her, furious at the thought of anyone disrespecting her. She's a goddess. Since the second I set eyes on her, she's had my cock hard, and my mind all twisted up. Her wide hips and thick thighs are sexy as hell to me. Her body is soft and ripe in all the right ways.

"Why?"

"I'm going to hunt down everyone who hurt you and teach them manners," I say, stopping in front of her. "Every last one of them."

Her expression softens, her gaze flitting across my face. She reaches up and gently taps me on the cheek with one finger. "Be careful," she says, her voice quiet... wistful. "I might start believing you mean it."

"You have ice cream on your cheek, sweet boy." My mom leans down to wipe chocolate off my cheek.

"Mom," I protest when she steals a lick of my cone. She always does. Even though she says she doesn't want any when she takes us for ice cream, she always ends up eating part of ours. It's why I always get chocolate instead of strawberry. It's her favorite.

Humor dances in her hazel eyes when she pulls back, her dimples cutting little grooves in her cheeks.

"You can have some of mine, mom." Nico holds his cone out for her, shrugging. Like me, my twin brother got chocolate too.

"That's very sweet of..." Mom's smile fades as a black car swerves around the corner, tires screeching. The windows are tinted dark like the ones on my dad's car, but it's older. The car bounces to a stop on the curb in front of us.

"Rafe, Nico, run," Mom says, urgency in her voice.

I turn to look at her, confused.

Out of the corner of my eye, I see the windows of the vehicle inch down.

"Run," Mom says again, louder this time. She grabs me and Nico, shoving us away from the car.

Nico trips, falling backward onto the sidewalk. His ice cream lands beside him, the chocolate spilling out of the cone.

"Run, baby!" Mom screams at me. "Run!"

Except it's already too late.

*Gunfire rips through the quiet neighborhood, tearing my life asunder.*

"Rafe." A hand clamps down on my shoulder, shaking me.

I react on instinct, adrenaline coursing through my veins. In one smooth move, my assailant is on the bed beneath me, my hand around his throat, my body pinning his to the bed. I snarl wordlessly, ready to kill this motherfucker. And then I see Amalia's wide chocolate eyes, her mouth open in shock. I feel her soft body beneath mine.

It's not an assailant. It's Amalia.

"Fuck," I snarl, flinging myself off her. I plaster my back to the wall, sucking in deep breaths. My heart races, images from the dream still clinging to me. No, not a dream. A living nightmare. The day my mom died. It's been twenty-seven years and I still relive that shit almost every night. I gave up trying to forget it long ago. Some things never go away. Some things never should.

"Are you okay?" Amalia asks, sitting up.

I make a choked sound, half crazed laugh, half tortured groan. I just had her pinned to the bed with my hand around her throat, and she's asking if *I'm* okay? No, I'm not. If I hurt her, I'll chain myself in hell beside my father. "Did I hurt you, *tesoro*?"

"I..."

*"Did I hurt you, Amalia?"*

"No," she says, shaking her head. Her hair is tangled around her face, her long pajamas all twisted up. She should look like a schoolmarm in the ridiculous flannel things, but she looks like a rumpled seductress. She's worn them the past two nights. "You just startled me." She blinks wide eyes at me. "Has anyone ever told you that you move like a freaking ninja?"

"A few times." I expel a sharp curse, scrubbing a hand through my hair. At least it's not shaking. I take another breath, trying to get myself under control. And then I cross back to the bed. "Let me see your throat."

"It's fine."

"Now, Amalia."

"Now, Amalia," she mimics, glaring at me. *"El burro sabe más que tú."*

*The donkey knows more than you.* I let her insult slide, not sure if she's realized yet that I speak Spanish fluently or if she's just venting to herself. With her, who knows? She's smart as hell. She also has a fiery temper and a fearless streak a mile wide.

She huffs and cranes her head back, allowing me to inspect her throat.

"No marks," I say. I was half convinced I was going to find bruises on her beautiful skin. The thought made what's left of my soul shrivel. I've seen—and done—things that would horrify most people, but the thought of causing this woman even a moment of pain feels like acid poured directly into my veins.

I don't want to harm this woman. Far from it. The longer I spend near her, the more I find myself wanting things I've never wanted until now. Things I've never allowed myself to want. When I made my deal with my father to free Nico, I left behind dreams of a normal life, of a wife and kids and love and companionship. I couldn't allow myself to want things that made me vulnerable. But they beckon now, whispering as if from the grave to remind me those desires aren't dead. I simply buried them alive. And they're no longer content to lie quietly.

Because of *her*. Because something about her makes me feel things I shouldn't, makes me crave a taste of freedom. She's consuming me, piece by piece, minute by minute. Where's the cold, calculated crime boss now? Where's the heartless, ruthless king now? Already, he's slipping away, replaced by someone I don't recognize. And yet I don't hate it. I...relish it.

Every electrifying moment.

She's been in my bed for two nights, slowly driving me mad. She tosses and turns, mumbling in her sleep. The row of pillows she diligently places between us each night taunts me, daring me to cast them aside and pull her into my arms. But I haven't. I've kept my hands to myself, clinging to honor by the skin of my teeth. I haven't touched her at all since that first day, trying to give her time to get used to me, to gain her trust.

"I told you I was fine," she mutters without heat.

I hesitate for a split second and then wrap my hand around her throat again, desperate to replace the memory of that harsh touch with something softer, something befitting a queen. She tenses for a moment, and then slowly melts into my touch, shivering.

My blood heats, my cock stirring back to life. She might not want to admit it, but she feels me too. She wants me too. Her eyes go glassy, the pulse in her throat jumping. I resist the urge to lean down and taste it on my tongue, fighting the bonds of obsession even though I want to fall backward into them.

*Slowly, slowly,* I remind myself. I'm a dying man, ready to drown myself in an oasis. But I can't run before I walk, or this will all blow up in my face.

"I have nightmares," I say...the closest thing to an apology I've ever given. My thumb makes circles against the tendon in the side of her neck. "Bad ones. You woke me from one."

"You were talking in your sleep." Her eyes seek mine in the lamplight. "You were talking about your mom, mumbling for her to run."

"I'd regret it for the rest of my life if I hurt you."

"Oh," she says, her throat working as she swallows hard. "Then I guess it's a good thing you didn't. Can I ask a question?"

I jerk my head in a nod.

"Were you there?" she whispers. "I mean the day she was murdered?"

"My twin brother and I were both there," I say, pushing down the memories that immediately bubble to the surface. They're too close tonight, still too raw. I release her throat and take a step back, lifting my shirt.

Her gaze falls to my abdomen, raking like wildfire. Everything it touches goes up in flames. Until she sees the scars.

"Rafe," she gasps, her expression stricken. She lifts a shaking hand, tracing her fingertips across the puckered flesh of my stomach. The heat of her hand sears me. How long has it been since I willingly let anyone touch me? I can't remember. "You were shot?"

"Twice."

A tear slips down her cheek, wrecking me. How can she cry for me? Why would she? I brought her here. I'm holding her here against her will. Ten minutes ago, I had her pinned to the bed. I'm the last person who deserves her tears, and yet she cries them for me anyway.

"Get some sleep, *tesoro*. It's late," I murmur, cupping her face in my palm. I steal her tears, rubbing them into my skin so she can't take them back. She cried them for me. They belong to me now.

"What about you?" Heat creeps into her cheeks. "I mean, you should try to sleep too."

Four hours ago, she threatened to smother me with a pillow like usual if I crossed onto her side of the bed. Now, she wants me back in the bed with her. Women are very confusing. This one most of all.

"Didn't you know, *mi reinita*?" I ask, leaning down to press my lips to hers in a quick kiss. "The devil does his best work in the dark."

I'm halfway to the door before she answers. "I'm *not* afraid of you, Rafe."

Perhaps she should be.

CHAPTER 4

*Amalia*

"Y ou aren't supposed to be out here alone."

I glance over my shoulder, my stomach sinking when I see Carmine Esposito leaning up against the wall behind me, grinning. His eyes are locked on me, the smirk on his face making my stomach turn. He's the same guard who creeped me out when I first arrived here four days ago. I don't feel any better about him now.

Every time I turn around, he's watching me. This is the first time he's tried to speak to me though. He usually keeps a polite distance. I think that's because Coda and Domani are always breathing down my neck. That's probably my fault for trying to run out the front door at every available opportunity, but Rafe can't say I didn't warn him.

It's not like he's even here anyway. He walked out of the bedroom two nights ago...and disappeared. He hasn't been back since.

"I'm not trying to run away," I mutter, rolling my

59

eyes at Carmine. I tried that earlier. All I got out of it was a twisted ankle. Besides, I doubt Coda and Domani are far. They tend to materialize out of thin air whenever I even think about trying to make a break for it. Its infuriating. And impressive. I'm pretty sure they were ninjas in a former life.

It's not hard to see why Rafe is the big boss in this city. He's a force to be reckoned with, and so are his men. They're intimidating as hell. Unfortunately for them, I don't intimidate easily. I grew up surrounded by violent men and the sound of gunfire. Diego and Alvise taught me how to protect myself long before I really understood that it wasn't even the gangs they were truly worried about. It was Rafe and his brothers. For them, it *was* always Rafe and his brothers.

I only now find myself wondering why. It's... disconcerting to come face-to-face with the enemy and realize that he's not the monster they said he was. He's not innocent, not even close. But he's a product of his environment, just like the rest of us. Part of him is still a terrified eleven-year-old boy who watched his mother die...who almost died himself. He's fighting to survive this world, just like the rest of us.

I can't hate him. I understand him all too well.

Carmine's smirk widens. He's handsome. At least, I'm sure most women think so. But there's something about him that just feels...off to me. It's the way he looks at me like he knows something I don't. I don't like it. No, I don't like *him*.

"How's your ankle?" he asks.

"Fine." I lift my legs out of the hot tub, swinging

them out onto the cement. My pants are rolled up to my knees. I quickly tug them down, not wanting this man to see any more of my skin than absolutely necessary. The fabric immediately sticks to my wet skin, but I don't care. At least I'm covered.

"You remind me of someone," he says, pushing away from the wall. He strolls toward me, his gaze flicking up and down my body. "This *balena* I went to school with for a while. Here, let me help you." He stops in front of me, holding out a hand to help me to my feet.

I hesitate, wanting to tell him no, but it's either accept his help or let him stare at my ass in the air when I roll to my knees. I quickly place my hand in his, letting him pull me to my feet. I expect him to let me go as soon as I'm standing, but he doesn't. He holds onto my hand for a moment, his head cocked to the side, still smirking.

"Except you can't be her," he murmurs. "Her name was Serafina Cerrito."

My heart stops beating. The blood freezes in my veins. For a long moment, time stands still. How many years has it been since I've heard that name? Nine? Ten? We buried her deep, hiding her so no one would ever find her. Except Carmine remembers her. *He knows.*

Panic beats at me, firing through my veins like mortar from a cannon. My muscles tense with the urge to run. I fight it off, refusing to give in. He might suspect, but he doesn't know. He's guessing. If he knew, he would have gone straight to Rafe and spilled my secrets. He wouldn't be out here, trying to goad me into a reaction.

"I've never heard of her," I say, proud when my voice doesn't waver. "But you should probably let go of my hand before Rafe finds out you touched me. I'd hate to learn you disappeared when you were just trying to be helpful."

He squints at me, something dark flashing in his eyes. For a minute, I think he's going to hang onto me anyway, but voices carry around the side of the house and he quickly releases me and takes a step back.

"See you around, Amalia."

I duck my head and hurry toward the house, shivering.

"There you are, *reginetta*," Mattia says, shooting a withering glare at Coda and Domani.

They shift restlessly from foot to foot, wearing matching expressions of guilt. Like Rafe, the men all treat Mattia with a healthy dose of respect. He calls the shots around here, second only to Rafe. Everyone jumps to obey him just like they do Rafe. They're more casually familiar with him than with Rafe, but no less quick to respond to an order.

"I didn't run off," I mumble. "I was just soaking my foot in the jacuzzi."

"Did it help?" Mattia looks genuinely worried.

"It's fine."

"Maybe I should call someone to come look at it," he says.

"It's fine."

"It wouldn't hurt to have someone look at it."

*"Ti corro in culo!"* I growl in Italian, flinging my hands up.

All three of them stare at me with wide eyes as I stomp past, headed for the library. Mattia doesn't press me about having a doctor look at my ankle again though. They leave me alone, allowing me to escape in silence to the library.

Once inside, I close the door, leaning back against it. My entire body trembles with fear. How does Carmine remember me? Is that why he looks familiar? We went to school together at some point? I wrack my brain, trying to place him. I come up with nothing. I changed schools so many times they all bleed together.

We knew there was a risk sending me here, but we were so sure it was minimal. That I'd been off the radar for so long no one would ever think to link me to the long-lost daughter of Alessandro Cerrito and his beloved Latina wife. Rafe can't ever find out the truth. My father didn't just murder his mother. He tried to kill him too.

Even now, Rafe still suffers because of it. The memories of that day still torment him.

If he ever finds out the truth...even if he doesn't kill me, he'll never forgive me.

*Oh, Amalia. You foolish, foolish girl. You're falling for him.*

"You've been giving my men trouble, *tesoro*."

I look up from my book to see Rafe standing in the doorway of the library, his expression tense. My stomach clenches as soon as my gaze lands on him, heat unfurling inside me. He looks good. Better than that, actually. A five o'clock shadow darkens his jaw, giving the razor-sharp plane a wicked edge.

"Sucks for them," I say, holding his gaze. It's been three days since I last saw him. If they didn't like dealing with me in his absence, too bad. Maybe next time, he'll think twice before kidnapping me and then making me someone else's problem.

"Did you miss me, Amalia?"

"You were gone?" I smile sweetly.

He narrows his eyes, moving into the room. "Don't piss me off, *tigrotta*."

I ignore him, going back to my book.

Two seconds later, it disappears from my hands.

"I was reading that."

"Sucks for you." He tosses it over his shoulder, caging me in on the window seat with his arms on either side of my head. His leather and brandy scent hits me, wreaking havoc on my system. Why does he have to smell so damn good?

I've fallen asleep covered in his scent every night since he brought me here. My dreams are full of him. It's making me crazy.

"How many times did you try to run away while I was gone?"

"They didn't tell you?" I ask, surprised. I assumed they were giving him reports of my half-hearted escape attempts. We all know there's no way I'm getting off this property unless Rafe lets me go, but I figure I have to at least try. Both to make them believe I don't want to be here, and because a not so little part of me is...hurt that Rafe just disappeared for three days without explanation.

It's stupid, of course. I'm just a means to an end to him. But part of me actually believed him when he said he'd regret it for the rest of his life if he hurt me. Part of me let myself believe that maybe, just maybe he cared about me. That part of me is a naive little girl.

I wake up every morning to some new gift from him, but I know he only sends them to keep me complacent. As if this is just a game to him and I'm just a pawn on the board. I'm not sure if I'm more pissed that he tries to play me...or if I'm more hurt that he just disappeared for three days without even saying goodbye.

"I want to hear it from you," he says.

"None."

"Liar." The smile in his voice threatens to thaw a little of the ice around my heart.

"One."

He arches a brow.

"Fine. Eleven. But I followed your stupid rule, so the terms of our agreement still stand," I say, praying no one told him that I twisted my ankle yesterday. If he tries to lock me up in his room again, I will smother him with a pillow. I've already checked it from top to bottom. There's nothing of use to me in there.

I'm not sure there's anything helpful in his office either. There aren't any guards on the door, and it's unlocked. I have a feeling any dirt he keeps here is hidden in the west wing, the one place I'm not allowed to go. After my run-in with Carmine yesterday, I'm a little afraid to even try sneaking into the west wing to poke around. The last thing I need to do is rouse his suspicion.

I have no idea what I'm doing. I just want to get out. This place, this man...they're dangerous to me in ways I didn't expect. Diego prepared me for war. He didn't teach me how to guard my heart. I'm no longer sure what we're even fighting for here. The whole thing seems so pointless. Diego wants to topple Rafe and the Valentino empire, but it seems to me that he suffers enough already.

I don't think he enjoys any of what he does. Nor do I think it's something he relishes. It's a weight on his shoulders, one he carries for reasons I don't yet understand. But he carries it anyway. Isn't that punishment enough for his crimes? Can I really sacrifice one man to save another?

Doubt plagues me, unsettling me.

"I missed you," Rafe says.

"Your willing bedmates weren't enough for you?" I snap, refusing to bend even if he does sound exhausted. *Especially* because he sounds exhausted.

"Willing bedmates?" His gaze seeks mine.

I turn my face to the side to avoid his. I didn't mean to say that. And I don't want to talk about it now that I have. The way I feel about this man isn't rational. It makes no sense. He's the enemy, the man who will kill my brother with no remorse and no hesitation. He's a murderer, a tyrant, and worse. But God help me, I want him anyway. The thought of him with anyone else eats me up with jealousy. I've thought of nothing else since he's been gone. Him kissing someone else. Him holding someone else. Him staking his claim on someone else. How many other women in this city are also *his*? How many know how intoxicating his kisses are?

I *hate* that I'm jealous. And I hate that I don't hate it at all. He's gotten under my skin and no amount of arguing with myself about it will expel him. If anything, it only seems to embed him a little deeper.

"Look at me, Amalia," he orders me.

"I don't take orders from you," I growl.

"Look at me."

"No."

His hand delves into my hair, pulling just hard enough to have my clit thrumming in time to my heart. I'm not afraid of him and he knows it. I think that's exactly why he does it, to remind me that I'm not afraid of him. To remind me how much I like it when he touches me. To remind me that I'm his, even if I hate it. Even when he pinned me to the bed the other night, caught in the throes of his nightmare, I wasn't afraid. Perhaps I should have been, but I wasn't.

"Look at me."

"No."

He encircles my throat with his free hand, moving slowly as if to give me time to tell him no. Except...I don't.

He squeezes gently.

I barely fight back a moan.

The second time he touched my throat the other night, I wanted him to squeeze like he is right now. I'm not sure what that says about me, and I don't care. He's the worst possible thing for me...and yet I'm *mad* that he left me here without a word. I'm angry that he forgot about me so easily when I've done nothing but obsess about him for three damn days.

I don't want to be one of many he calls his. I want to be the *only* one.

I'm acting like a jealous brat because I *am* a jealous brat. He turned me into one.

"Look at me."

"Go to hell."

"I've been there for twenty years, *tesoro*."

"Let me go." I kick out with my foot, aiming for his shin. He evades me with embarrassing ease.

"You're asking for it, little girl," he growls.

The hairs on my arms rise at the feral sound. My clit

thrums harder, screaming for attention he won't give it. Not unless I give him what he wants. Not unless I submit, and hand over my soul. It's shameful how quickly freedom loses its luster when he's looming over me like a dangerous animal pushed too far.

"Let me go," I whisper again, a wisp of sound that hangs in the air between us.

"Never," Rafe growls, unholy fire and unwavering certainty turning his eyes to molten chocolate. "I will never let you go, Amalia. How many times do I have to tell you? You're mine, *mi reinita. Sono debole per te.*"

*I'm weak for you.*

"Rafe," I whimper, cracking like Humpty Dumpty falling from his wall. And just like with Humpty Dumpty, I *know* all the way to my soul that there will be no putting me back together again. This is it for me. Once I fall into his hands, he'll own me, body and soul.

I've never wanted anything more.

*Forgive me, Diego. Oh God, forgive me.*

Rafe pulls me to my feet, seaming our bodies together—soft on hard. "There are no bedmates, *tesoro*," he says, tipping my head back until our eyes meet. His blaze with fervent promise. "There's only you. There will only *ever* be you. Understand?"

I understand. My soul cries out in understanding, shaking me all the way to my foundation. It's profound, the shift that promise sets off inside me. A landslide of sensation threatens to consume me, emotion tangled so tightly together I don't stand a chance of picking them apart now. So I don't try.

I lift up on my toes, pressing my mouth to his. I

don't want to talk right now. I don't want to think about this beautiful, complicated man handing me his heart. I don't want to consider how very little I deserve it or what it all means or what happens next. Right now, I don't want to *think* at all. I just want to feel.

Rafe growls my name, backing me toward the sofa. My knees hit the cushions and I fall backward onto the plush top. He follows me down, his hands tangling in my hair. I cry out in bliss as his body covers mine.

"Ah, *tesoro*," he groans, wedging one leg roughly between mine. "I've spent three nights in hell, thinking of you alone in my bed. And you question if I was with another? My cock will be your throne, *mi reinita*. Yours."

"Rafe," I sob.

"I smell you, *tesoro*. So sweet. So pure." He consumes me all over again, just like he did that first day. Only it's even better this time, even hotter. He kisses me like he doesn't ever plan to stop. His hands in my hair sting and don't sting enough. His tongue works against mine, sending me spiraling into an erotic frenzy that's unlike anything I've ever felt.

No, this man isn't cold and controlled. When he's kissing me, he's the exact opposite. He's burning hot, as desperate and out of control as I am. And yet he controls me with frightful ease. I find myself *wanting* to submit and cede jurisdiction of my soul to him.

I cry out in loss when he pulls away to kiss a trail down my throat.

"Shh," he whispers, nipping at my collarbone. His

tongue dips into the hollow before he moves lower. His teeth close around my nipple in a sharp bite.

My entire body bows off the couch, my mouth open in a silent cry of ecstasy. My clit pulses so hard I feel it everywhere, as if every nerve ending in my body fires with it.

I want to beg him to do it again, but he doesn't give me a chance. He moves lower, his dark head bent over my stomach. He places his lips to my belly, making it quiver and dance beneath his touch. Even through my top, his touch sears me. It's intimate, gentle, almost...worshipful.

"*Bellissima*," he breathes, he chocolate eyes scorching. I don't doubt he means it. I can't. He finds me and all my flaws beautiful. To him, I'm not fat or a whale or any of the things other men call me. I'm perfect. I think he would hunt down everyone who ever called me names if I'd let him.

He moves lower, dragging my skirt up my hips. He keeps his gaze locked on mine, holding me captive. I don't breathe. I can't. I don't stop him either. I don't *want* to stop him. Whatever he's about to do to me, I want it. Desperately.

"Oh, *tesoro*," he says, slowly lowering his gaze when my skirt is around my waist, exposing my panties to the room. "Did kissing me make this mess of your panties, or did fighting me?"

"I..."

"Tell me."

"Both," I whisper, the hardest word I've ever said. And perhaps the truest. Fighting him turns me on.

Whatever that says about me, well, maybe it's not good. I don't know, but it's the truth. I'm no man's plaything, no man's obedient little toy. I've never even been touched before. But the same fire that fuels him runs in my veins too. My mother was Latina. My father Italian. He was Mafioso just like Rafe. I may not remember them, but I'm their daughter. All the way to the core.

"Look at me, Amalia."

I reluctantly meet his gaze, half afraid of the judgment I'll see there. Only...there's nothing but understanding reflected back at me. As if he knows exactly how I feel. As if he feels it too. But he can't, can he?

"Make me earn every drop of honey you spill for me," he growls. "Sharpen your claws in my back. Fight me as hard and as often as you want, *tigrotta*. Because when it's my turn to play, I intend to fuck the fight right out of you."

My stomach clenches, a loud moan breaking from my lips before I can call it back. He means it. And God help us both, but I want him to do exactly that. Except...

"I'm a virgin, Rafe," I whisper, the second hardest thing I've ever said. Letting this man see my vulnerabilities when I know he could use them against me is terrifying in a way being here isn't. The more walls I knock down for him, the more I stand to lose here. If I am just a pawn for him to move about the board, he could easily destroy me.

"No one has ever touched you, Amalia?"

"Never."

Hellfire lights his eyes again. For the first time, he

gives me a real smile. One so pure and so purely wicked, it steals my breath and a piece of my heart.

"Oh, *tesoro*," he breathes. "I'm going to enjoy corrupting you." He dips his head, placing a kiss on my belly, and then he slides off the side of the sofa, landing on his knees beside it.

Before I can ask any questions, his hands lock around my hips, gently turning me. My legs fall off the couch, splaying on either side of his body. He quickly lifts them over his shoulders, placing kisses on my inner thighs.

I tremble at his touch, full of nerves and nervous anticipation.

"W-what–" My tongue feels thick and cloven to the roof of my mouth. My heart pounds, beating in time to the pulse of my clit.

"Am I going to do to you?" he asks, finishing the sentence when I can't.

I nod.

"I'm going to see how hard you fight when you're desperate to come, Amalia." His wicked, heavy-lidded gaze meets mine. "And then I'm going to take you to heaven."

*Oh my God.*

He leans forward, nuzzling his nose against my center. I startle beneath him, and then startle again when he breathes deeply, smelling me like he's a wild animal scenting prey.

"Goddamn," he growls, his hands tightening on my thighs. "I'm going to eat you alive, *tesoro*."

"Please," I plead, though I'm not sure what exactly

I'm begging for here. Him to get on with it? Mercy? I don't know. I just need...something. Otherwise, I'm going to burst apart at the seams.

I don't even care if anyone could walk in and catch us at any moment. Something tells me he wouldn't allow them to see a single part of me like this even if they did walk in. Would I even care if they did? All I care about is this moment, this man, and the piercing, crippling ache raging through me like a storm.

Rafe flicks his tongue out, touching it to the seam of my panties. The sound he makes then isn't human. It's also loud enough to shake the heavens. He practically roars, bellowing as the last thread of his control snaps in half.

He moves like lightning striking, yanking my ass off the edge of the couch. My panties rip down the center, exposing me to him. I feel his fiery, hungry gaze on me, looking where no one ever has before, seeing what no one has ever seen.

Another savage growl rips from his throat. His eyes are on fire, blazing like two black suns. I get caught in them, pulled into their orbit. So much swirls there, things I can't even begin to understand. It's light and dark, heaven and hell. Something inside me rises in response, some part of me I've never met yet know all too well. She's wanton and wild, as wicked as this man.

"I thought you were going to take me to heaven." The challenge rolls off my tongue without thought. "I'm still waiting."

The heat in his eyes intensifies. "Don't interrupt me while I'm eating, Amalia."

"You aren't eat– Rafe!" I scream, startled when he lunges. He lands face first in my center, licking me from the bottom to the top. His hands are vises around my hips, holding me down as powerful sensations blast through me.

Oh my God. *Oh my God.*

Rafe snarls exactly like the dangerous beast he is. A maelstrom rages to life inside me, threatening to unmake me with every swipe of his tongue. He isn't going to claim my soul. He's going to possess it. And God help me, I'll let him do it. Even if it destroys us both. Even if it destroys *everything*.

I grip his hair, pulling, pushing...fighting like hell to bring him closer and push him away at the same time. I shout his name, clawing at his shoulders. He pulls my clit into his mouth, sucking like he never intends to stop.

I sob in ecstasy. It's so good, so good. Ah, God. What is he doing to me? My feet dig into his upper back, the heels finding the brawny muscles of his shoulders.

"That's it," he snarls against my pussy. "Fight me, *tesoro*. Make me work like a fucking dog for it."

He spreads my cheeks apart, burying his face deeper. I feel him everywhere. And I still want more. What does that say about me? That I want to bring this giant to his knees? That I want to be the one who leaves him trembling?

I don't want him to be Rafael Valentino, *Capo dei capi*, with me. I just want him to be mine. My dark prince. My wicked captor. My king. No armor. No masks. Just *mine*.

"Rafe!" I scream, clawing down his arms as a powerful orgasm blooms in my stomach, setting me ablaze. I go up like kindling, all at once. It happens so fast it knocks me breathless and leaves me reeling.

Waves crest and crash over me again and again, battering me against the shores of submission. Rafe curses and snarls, eating me loud and messy. He doesn't even let me come down before he's dragging me up the cliff again, ruthlessly driving me toward a second orgasm.

I fight for real this time, afraid of the immense cliff looming. It's even bigger than the first. There's no way I'm going to survive it. No way. I thrash in his hold, trying to buck him off me.

He flips me onto my stomach with embarrassing ease, handling me like I'm a little girl instead of a grown woman. His hand comes down on my ass in a sharp smack that surprises me more than anything.

"You can take it, Amalia," he says.

"I can't."

He wraps my hair in a gentle fist, craning my head back until my wild eyes meet his. "You made a rope of my clothes and tried to climb down to freedom," he says. "Twelve of my best soldiers live in fear of that smart mouth and the plans forming behind those mocha eyes. Do not tell me you can't take it. You're a fucking *queen*. You were made to be pleasured."

Well, put that way.

"I-I'm scared," I admit, feeling vulnerable and

exposed and raw. God, so raw. What is he doing to me? And why don't I want him to stop?

"I'll catch you," he whispers, leaning forward to brush his mouth across mine. I taste myself on his lips, and I don't hate it.

I nod bravely, giving him my trust, and another little piece of my heart.

"Sit up, *tesoro*," he says, rising to his feet. He helps me sit, and then pulls me to my knees, draping me over the back of the sofa.

I hear the soft growl of his zipper as he releases it, and then the rustle of fabric. A moment later, the sofa dips as he kneels behind me, his chest to my back. I melt against him, moaning quietly. The soft fabric of his suit and the warmth of his hard body beneath is an erotic dichotomy against my body.

"Together this time, *mi reinita*," he says, sweeping my hair to the side to nuzzle his face into my throat. "Lift up a little."

I obediently lift up onto my knees. He locks one arm around my waist. The other rucks my skirt up, exposing my ass. Only then do I feel his massive erection against my bare skin.

"Rafe," I gasp.

"I'm not going to fuck you," he murmurs, his mouth against my ear. "When you give yourself to me the first time, it'll be in our bed, *tesoro*. Your virgin blood will stain our sheets. Right now, I just want to feel you dripping on my cock when you come."

I tremble in his arms, and then nod.

He lifts me slightly, slipping his erection between

my legs. My head falls forward, my neck losing power when I feel it against my center. God, he's big and hard everywhere. The broad head bumps my clit, making us both moan.

Even though I'm not a small girl, I *feel* small with him draped over me like this. It's as if the rest of the world ceased to exist the moment he touched me. All that's left is him and us.

He reaches around me, sliding his hand down my stomach. My breath grows choppy, my skin hot. I quiver in anticipation, already aching to go over.

"*Bellissima*," he whispers in my ear, tonguing the shell of it. "*Bellissima*."

I cry out when his thumb touches my clit. He rubs in slow circles, rocking his hips at the same time so his cock glides through my drenched folds. He keeps his body pressed to mine, keeping me draped over the back of the couch. His lips and tongue wreak havoc on me, seeking out every sensitive place on my throat.

Something, some instinct or desire to make him feel even half of what he's making me feel, has me pressing my legs together, forcing him to push his erection through a tighter space.

He growls my name, nipping my throat. "You want to wear my cum today, *tesoro*?"

"M-maybe."

He nips me again. "Then work your hips for me, Amalia. Move with me."

It takes me a minute to work out the rhythm, but when I do, we move together, rocking into each other, sliding against one another. He kisses all over my neck, groaning encouragement in my ear. His hand between my legs drives me crazy, and then crazier.

I writhe beneath him, squirming in agonized bliss. It's beyond perfect. I'm a little afraid to know how much better it can possibly get. Because he's not even inside me and I'm already addicted. How am I going to survive it when he finally *is* inside me?

"Rafe," I moan. "I'm...I'm..." I grip his free hand, squeezing as the orgasm starts to wash through me.

"Come," he growls in my ear. "Drip all over my cock, Amalia. Mark it as yours, *mi reinita*."

I cry out his name, slumping over as it hits. The room falls out of focus. Fireworks dance behind my eyes, lighting my world up in vivid, blinding color.

Rafe grips my hip. He rocks against me, his erection bumping against my clit in steady taps that send tremors through my entire body. He curses and grunts, and then falls still.

"Amalia." My stomach bottoms out, an aftershock blowing through me as he rasps my name, his voice rough and gritty. He shudders, and then his erection jerks. Wetness spills between my legs. No, not wetness. Him.

He releases again and again, warm ropes of his cum spilling across my center and inner thighs. It drips down my legs onto the sofa, making a mess. It's beautiful.

He's right. This is heaven.

"*Mi reinita*," he breathes, falling forward. His body pins mine to the couch. His lips touch the side of my neck in a reverent kiss. "God. You light my world up with color and bring me to life."

"Rafe," I whisper. "I–"

Loud footsteps cut me off.

Rafe tenses, shifting to block me from view. "Get the fuck out," he snarls. There isn't a trace of the sweet man who just told me that I light up his world and bring him to life. The devil is back, as cold and ruthless as ever. And yet he still holds me tenderly, as if I'm priceless.

"Sorry, boss," Mattia says apologetically from behind us. "But there's a situation."

"*Mafankulo.*"

"Genovese wants a sit-down."

"I'll be out in a minute."

Mattia's footsteps retreat. A moment later, the door closes with a soft click.

"You're having dinner with me tonight," Rafe says a moment later.

"Is that a command?"

"With you? Never, *tesoro*," he promises, pressing a kiss to my temple. "It's a plea."

"In that case, I suppose I'll have dinner with you," I say, smiling to myself.

He chuckles and then regretfully peels himself off me. A moment later, he smooths my skirt down over my ass, and then cranes my head back. "Go straight upstairs and put on clean panties, Amalia."

I don't have to ask to know this is an order. Nor am I crazy enough to argue. It's not my life at risk if I defy him. It's every man in this house who will pay the price of my defiance. I see the truth glittering in his eyes.

He is who he is...and I think part of him hates himself for it.

God. This beautiful, broken man.

No one told me that the real enemy here would be my own heart. And I'm pretty sure it already fell right into his hands.

T ommaso Genovese is old school Mafioso, a gangster from an era that ended before the internet was little more than a pipe dream, let alone a reality. People assume that makes him less dangerous. They're wrong. Tommaso had a thirst for power and a taste for blood before my father was out of diapers. He's a viper, as quick and merciless at seventy as he was at thirty-five.

He bows not because he's defeated but because he was smart enough to see what others didn't. Strength, real strength, means knowing when to fight, and when to concede. His family has survived every major shake-up and shakedown for the last half century because he knows when to be the hammer and when to be the nail.

Right now, he could be either.

"I heard a rumor today," he says, staring at me across the table of the small deli situated halfway between my territory and his. It's neutral ground, the only place we meet. There is no one else here except

83

Mattia and Tommaso's consigliere, Battista. To bring anyone else would show weakness. Tommaso may be old, but he's far from weak. Intelligence blazes in his eyes. His broad shoulders are straight, his head held high.

"Apparently there are a lot of those," I murmur, sipping my brandy. "I've been told they say I'm a murderous fiend who gets off on terrorizing people."

Tommaso smiles at that. I'm sure he's heard the same rumors about himself. Though, they're more accurate when it comes to him. He enjoys inflicting pain. He always has. I do what's necessary. At least I did. Now, I'm not so sure.

"They say your lawyer is on the lam," he says.

"That one is new." We talk around the truth, never lying outright to one another. It's our way. There is no honor in deceit. But I learned long ago to live in that gray area between truth and deceit. My lawyer is on the lam, but the rumor is new. I didn't deceive, nor did I confirm.

"Mmhmm." Tommaso watches me like a hawk, looking for a crack, anything he can use. "They say you were spotted in gang territory looking for him."

I take another sip of brandy, giving nothing away. I can't tell him that Diego betrayed me, just like he won't ask if I'm after his territory. We'll give each other nothing the other could potentially use, nothing that might threaten our thrones. This game is as old as time. Every word I speak, he'll pick apart, look at from every angle. He'll try to find a hole, anything he can use. I'll do the same.

I've gotten good at this game too. My father was a master at it. He taught me well. I'd rather hang myself with my chains than play another round of this fucking game right now. Actually, I'd rather be at home, wrapped around Amalia than play this fucking game. But I play it anyway.

Why?

I'm not sure I even know anymore. No, that's not true. I do it for Gabe and Luca, and for Nico. To ensure their safety. If not for them, I would have let this empire crumble long ago. There is no leaving the mafia, no life after *Omertà*. Genovese and men like him stay their hands only because they know they can't beat me. If they could, my brothers would live with targets on their backs. It wouldn't end until every one of us were dead.

"I was in gang territory," I say eventually, giving him a partial truth, the parts I'm sure he's already confirmed. "I picked up something that belongs to me."

"The girl." He cracks a smile, and I know I just gave the wily bastard exactly what he was after.

*Mafankulo*. So that's what this is really about. Amalia. I want to smash my glass into his smug fucking face. Instead, I force myself to relax back in my seat, striving for calm. I don't want this motherfucker to know a goddamn thing about her or how I feel about her.

"She's yours," he says.

*I'll kill you and everyone you love if you touch her.*

"Why so interested in who warms my bed, Tommaso?" I ask, arching a brow. "Sofia would gut you in your sleep." Everyone knows he doesn't fuck around on his wife. She's a little firecracker of a woman who leads him around by the balls.

"I know the rules, Rafael," he says, unoffended. He gives me a shrewd, assessing look. "Your father was *un gran' disgraziato*. Our women were always meant to be off-limits, but he didn't listen to reason. I always suspected you'd be the one to take his place."

I eye him levelly, not sure where he's going with this.

"You understand family in a way he never did," Tommaso says. "It's the only reason I'm telling you this now. There's a rumor. Someone is offering a lot of money for the girl."

"Who?" I growl.

Tommaso shrugs. "It could be just a rumor. But my Sofia sleeps easy at night again. This girl deserves the same chance. We protect what belongs to us."

I jerk my chin in a nod, my heart pounding. I'll fucking kill anyone who even thinks about coming for her. But I don't say that. I can't. I know he sees it in my eyes though. There's no hiding it. I'm in love with her. Pretty soon, everyone will know it.

"*Grazie,*" I mutter, draining my brandy.

"What do you think?" Mattia asks once we're safely inside the Bentayga, headed toward the house.

"I don't know," I murmur, staring blankly out the window. "He told me for a reason."

"You didn't give him much."

I grunt. We both know I gave him more than enough to confirm she's important to me. Tommaso has been playing this game longer than anyone else. I gave him everything he needed. But will he use it? That's the real question.

He meant what he said about his wife, but I can't count on his gratitude staying his hand. Not with Diego out there dropping bodies all over his territory and leaving a trail that leads right to my fucking door.

I clench my hands, breathing deeply to keep my temper in check. The urge to tear Diego apart rises fast and hot. He's causing me far too many fucking problems. Right now, he's not even my biggest concern.

Hell, he doesn't even rate. But he's the enemy I know. He's the one with a face. Whoever is after Amalia is an unknown, a shadow in the dark.

I want to find him and kill him slowly. If it's Genovese, he's a fucking idiot. He signed his own death warrant back there. Does he know it? Was that his plan? To get me to make the first move? If so, it might just work. No one will threaten Amalia. No one.

"I need you to chase down this fucking rumor," I tell Mattia through gritted teeth. "Find out if there's any validity to it or if he's just trying to get me to make the first move. Bring me whoever is responsible." I meet his gaze. "I want him alive, Mattia." Whether it's Genovese or someone else, they'll die by my hand.

"I'll need Coda."

"Fine. I'll put Vito on Amalia."

Mattia snorts. "She's still pissed at him for looking at her underwear. Besides, he gets distracted. She'll slip past him and be halfway up the back wall before he notices she's missing."

"She climbed the wall?"

"Nah, she hasn't gotten that far. She doesn't run very fast." He grimaces. "Full disclosure. Coda and Domani lost track of her for about fifteen minutes yesterday. Carmine found her soaking her ankle in the hot tub."

I pinch the bridge of my nose, my blood pressure rising all over again. "Why was she soaking her ankle?"

"She twisted it trying to escape."

"Why the fuck am I just hearing about this?" I

growl, dropping my hand to glare at my oldest friend. "You couldn't keep her in one piece for three days?"

"I believe the issue was that you were gone," he mutters, rubbing a hand down his face to hide a smile. "Next time you decide to punish yourself by banishing yourself from her presence, you might think about cluing her in first. I believe you hurt her feelings."

"Fuck." I didn't banish myself from her presence. Not exactly. I spent every fucking night sitting outside the house, watching over her, making sure she was safe. And every damn day talking to a shrink of sorts, trying to work my shit out.

I can't hurt her. I *won't*. If I have to talk through that day with every shrink in this city to exorcise it from my mind, that's what I'll do. Whatever it takes to ensure I'm not a danger to her in our bed.

"She missed you," he says. "And that pissed her off." He laughs quietly. "Judging from the scene I walked in on today, I guess she forgave you."

"We're working on it." A smile tugs at my lips at the memory, soothing the worst of my temper. God, she's incredible. I can't wait until I'm inside her, buried so deep she feels me everywhere. I already know she's going to blow my mind. She blew it today.

What would the people of this city say if they knew how easily I fell at her feet? This is my kingdom, and yet I'd hand it to her without a fucking word if she asked it of me. I'm not just in love with her, I'm obsessed with her. Completely. Irrevocably. I'm not going to make her my queen. I'm going to make her my fucking world.

"It's been a long time since I saw that." Mattia nods at me, indicating the smile. "It looks good on you."

"Been a long time since I had a reason to smile."

"She's good for you."

"Can I be good for her?" I ask quietly, the same question I've been wrestling with for the last three days. I'm not. There's no denying that. I'm probably the worst thing for her. But she makes me want to be someone worthy of her. For the first time in a long time, I want more than this.

I've spent two decades meticulously defending and building my father's empire. I've kept my word and then some. I've kept my brothers safe, even though it cost me my twin. Nico lives in the same city yet hasn't spoken a word to me in years. He doesn't speak to Gabe and Luca either, not if he can help it. I've amassed a fortune and then some.

For her, I'll burn it all to the fucking ground.

"The Rafe I know already is," Mattia says.

I glance at him.

"It doesn't have to be all or nothing, brother. It never had to be that way. Let her know the man I know," he says with a shrug. "That man has always been more good than anything, even if he was hellbent on proving otherwise."

I jerk my chin in a nod, grateful for the thousandth time for him and his counsel.

"Put Carmine on her," he suggests. "At least he pays attention."

Half an hour later, we walk into chaos.

Mattia and I both stop in the doorway, staring in shock as Amalia stands on the stairs, casually ordering my men about. Coda and Domani are nailing a family portrait above the mantel. Carmine and Vito are replacing lamps on the end tables. Zeno, Leone, and Mario wrestle a bookshelf into place in the living room. Antonio has a broom, attacking bits of dust with it. Marco is arranging flowers in a vase. There's an Afghan over the back of the sofa and a stack of books on the coffee table. Aside from the portrait, none of it belongs to me.

"Oh, hey," Amalia says, smiling brightly when she sees us. She practically dances down the stairs toward us, her tits bouncing in her shirt. "You would get here once the hard work is done."

"I wasn't aware we were doing any work, *tesoro*," I murmur, humor in my voice.

"Well, I'm not sure if you're aware of this either, but

you basically live in a mausoleum," she says, wrinkling her nose in distaste. "It's cold and sad."

"Is it?" I reach for her when her feet hit the landing, reeling her in toward me. I don't give a fuck if my men are watching us. Let them. She's mine. I'll touch her whenever I want, wherever I want.

"We won't tell anyone you asked your designer for emo-chic," she says, patting me on the cheek.

I dig my fingers into her ribs, making her squeal with laughter.

Zeno startles, dropping his end of the bookcase.

Jesus. This place is like a mausoleum if a little laughter startles them. At least it was. It feels more like a home with Amalia in it than it has since my mother died. There's warmth here for the first time in twenty-seven years.

"I'm just kidding!" she cries.

"No, you aren't."

"No, I'm not," she agrees, laughing up at me. "Your house is depressing."

Fuck, she's beautiful.

I tip my head down, claiming her mouth in a hard kiss. She moans quietly, melting into me. Her soft body lands against mine, my dick raging to life. I wrap my arms around her, turning her so no one can see her like this. I kiss her until my raw nerves settle and then I reluctantly break off, unwilling to get carried away with her here and now.

I'm a jealous, possessive bastard. I'll own it. This part of her is mine.

Her mocha eyes flutter open, wide and glassy. Her cheeks stained pink. Her lips swollen from my kisses.

"*Bellissima*," I growl, my cock throbbing.

Her sweet smile damn near brings me to my knees.

Who is trying to get their hands on her? Who do I need to kill?

"She can change anything she wants to change," I say, raising my voice to ensure everyone in the living room hears me.

Her eyes light up. "What if I want to paint the place hot pink?"

"Do you?" I wouldn't put it past her, not because she has a particular affinity for the color, but simply to see if I'd let her get away with it. She likes testing her boundaries, likes to see how far I'm willing to let her go. This world is new to her. *I'm* new to her. I don't think she has any idea yet that there's very little I wouldn't do to please her.

All she really knows of me is the bullshit Diego has filled her head with and the rumors she's heard on the streets. I won't lie to her and say they aren't true. Like she said, there's a kernel of truth in most rumors. More than I'd like to admit, especially to her. But I'm just a man. When it comes to her, I'm fucking weak. That doesn't shame me.

But it does worry me. Already, my enemies plot to use her against me. I'll leave Chicago in ruins before I let it happen. She may be bringing me back to life, but I'm still the motherfucker this city loses sleep over. As soon as I find out who put a price on her head, I'll make an example of them no one will forget.

"Not particularly." She grins at me.

"Change whatever you want to change, *mi reinita*," I say softly, rubbing my thumb over her bottom lip. "This stopped being a home twenty-seven years ago. Maybe it's time to make it one again."

"When your mom died," she says, her expression softening with understanding. Her gaze flits to the portrait Coda and Domani just hung. "Maybe I shouldn't have demanded they hang it. I just found it and thought...."

"Leave it, Amalia. She deserves a place here."

Amalia smiles at me, her bright eyes and the pride in them melting another block of ice from around my heart. Yes, it still beats. For her.

"Come." I reach for her hand, lacing our fingers together. "I promised you dinner. Let's go see what kind of damage you can do in the kitchen."

"I can cook," she says.

"Good to know." I lift her hand to my lips, brushing a kiss across her knuckles. I doubt there's much she can't do. "But what kind of jailer would I be if I made you cook, *tesoro*?"

"Can you cook?" She casts a suspicious look at me, her eyes narrowed.

"Can I cook?" I scoff. "I'm Italian."

"Really?" She blinks wide, innocent eyes at me, giving me a smile so full of sugar, I know she's up to no good. "And here I thought you were French this whole time. Quick. Someone alert the media! Rafael Valentino runs the Italian mafia, not the French mafia!"

"Jesus Christ," Mattia mutters behind us.

Everyone else falls completely silent. They don't even seem to breathe.

I stare at her for a long moment and then laugh loudly. There isn't another woman in this city who would have the nerve to call me out so boldly, so freely. There aren't many men who would either. They might whisper it behind their hands, but they'd never have the balls to say it to my face. Amalia though...Amalia isn't like anyone else in this city. She's unlike anyone anywhere. This curvy little queen is utter fucking perfection.

"Let's go, smart ass," I say, smiling indulgently. "I'm about to show you just how Italian I am."

## CHAPTER 6

*Amalia*

"**C**an I ask you a question?"

"You can ask me anything." Rafe smiles against my throat, his hands drifting through my hair. We're seated on a sofa on one of the back patios, the remnants of our dinner—an amazing mushroom gnocchi that Rafe cooked—on the table before us, the grounds of his estate sprawling out around us. The sun sinks slowly toward the horizon, setting the sky ablaze with color.

Rafe has his shirt sleeves rolled up, his tie undone. He's relaxed. So am I, for that matter. It's hard not to be when he's been working his magic on my body for the last two hours...touching me, kissing me, showering me with affection and compliments.

Rafael Valentino is a charming, wicked man. I think this is who he is beneath the mask of cold indifference he wears to survive his world. This is the man he could have been had his life turned out differently...the one he keeps locked away, hidden from everyone. Oddly though, this isn't the man I'm falling in love with. At least not entirely.

I'm falling hard for *both* sides of him. The ruthless, autocratic king who takes what he wants without apology and the tender, affectionate lover who worships the ground I walk on. One sets my blood on fire with need. The other makes my knees weak with desire. I want both sides of him.

If that makes me selfish, I'll own it.

"Your twin," I say haltingly, not sure how to broach this subject. When I found the portrait, Coda and Domani seemed more worried about his reaction to Nico than to his mom. Whatever happened between them was big. And clearly unhealed. "What happened between the two of you?"

Rafe tenses for a moment and then slowly relaxes. "Our father," he says, pulling back. His eyes meet mine, hard and dark. Full of ancient pain. "Nico was always more like our mom, always too fucking smart to be stuck here. Our father had other plans. He wanted an heir. Neither of us wanted to follow in his footsteps, but he was willing to play dirty to get what he wanted."

I slip my hand into his, squeezing gently. Maybe it's wrong to think ill of the dead, but I can't help but think it of Lorenzo Valentino.

"Nico got a full-ride to Harvard," he says. "He wanted me to go with him." He glances out at the grounds, his shoulders slumped as if a great weight rests on them. "We wanted out so fucking badly, but I knew there was no way our father would willingly let us both go. So the day before we turned eighteen, I made him a deal. My future for Nico's freedom."

"Rafe," I whisper, stunned.

"I don't regret it, *tesoro*," he says, his voice flat. "Nico never forgave me for choosing our father over him, but I'd make the same choice. I'd turn myself into this all over again to keep him out of our father's hands." He turns back to me, hellfire burning in his eyes. "I'm not a good man, Amalia. I'm everything the rumors say. But he isn't. I made sure he'll never have to be."

"You miss him."

"He's free," he says, his voice soft. I see the regret in his eyes though. The longing. He misses his twin a great deal. "That's all that matters."

"You don't think he would have survived, do you?" I ask, watching him intently, trying to understand. He sacrificed so much for his twin, but I don't think he did it to keep him from having to live *this* life. I think he did it to keep him alive, period.

"He wasn't made for this life, Amalia," he answers, his jaw tight, and I know that I'm right. That's what he really feared. Losing his twin like he lost his mom. My stomach ties itself in knots, my heart ripping itself to shreds as I realize that's always been the force that drives him. "This life is kill or be killed. That's not something he could have lived with. I can. I do. To protect my family, I'll chain my own soul in hell if that's what it takes."

The quiet intensity in his voice is unmistakable. He means it. He didn't rise to the top because he wanted to be there. He fought and killed his way to the top to make his family untouchable. To keep his brothers safe the only way he knew how. In this world, fear is power. And Rafael Valentino has a whole lot of both. No one crosses him. No one defies him. They wouldn't dare.

Until now.

Until Diego.

Until...me.

God. When he finds out why I'm here, he's going to hate me.

Somehow, I have to find a way to end this. He's suffered enough already. Every day, he suffers still. I can't add to it. I *won't*. But I don't know how I'm supposed to stop this either.

The man I love and my brother are runaway trains on a collision course. And I'm standing in the middle. To save Diego, I have to sacrifice Rafe. To save Rafe, I have to sacrifice Diego. Neither of them will back down. Neither of them will concede. Until Diego is dead or Rafe's empire crumbles, they won't stop now.

How can they?

They both have too much to lose.

*Please, God*, I pray. *Please help me find a way to end this before anyone gets hurt.*

Shaking, I climb to my feet and then step in front of Rafe. He leans back, looking up at me through dark lashes, every inch the king. But I see the cracks in his armor now, the thin spots where the steel isn't quite as thick. His nerves are raw, his shoulders tense.

I crawl into his lap, straddling his thighs.

His hands settle on my hips, his lips curving up at the corners. "What are you up to now, *tigrotta?*"

I desperately need him to make me his, but I don't say that.

"Well," I say, looping my arms around his neck and sliding down his thighs. I bite my lip, fighting back a moan at the glide of fabric and the thickness of his thighs against my bare skin. I'm still in a skirt. They're what I wear most days. I may be big, but the world can just deal with it. I refuse to hide behind baggy clothes and the weight of their shame. "I was thinking."

"About?" He slips his hands beneath my skirt, palming my ass. One fingertip skims along the band of my panties, teasing me.

"You gave me something I want," I murmur. "I should give you something you want."

"Yeah? I want you bouncing on my cock and screaming my name." He smirks, one brow arched. "Preferably with my hand around your pretty throat. I know how much you liked that this morning."

I moan quietly.

His smirk grows, his fingers digging into the cheeks of my ass. "Or maybe I'll take you face down so I can watch this ass bounce while I'm bottoming out in you. Tell me, Amalia, how hard do you think I can fuck you before you break?"

Not very. Not if he's going to use that wicked mouth and his filthy words.

"Depends," I say, leaning forward like I'm going to kiss him. I bring my mouth right up to his, until I feel his uneven breath pelting my lips. Something wholly wicked prompts me to flick my tongue out to touch his lip before I turn my head, denying him the kiss he silently demands. I kiss a trail along his jaw instead, slowly driving him crazy.

By the time I reach his ear, he's rigid and tense beneath me, his fingers gripping me hard enough to leave marks in my skin. I hope they do. I want a reminder of the moment I brought this man to his knees.

"On what?" he snarls.

"On how hard you want me to fight," I breathe before biting his neck. Hard.

He bellows my name like a bear, only he's not wounded. Not even close. I know that sound. I made the same one earlier today. It's ecstasy. This wicked, beautiful man likes it rough and dirty. And as it turns out, so do I.

It's freeing to know I'm not alone in this storm. That the maelstrom raging in my veins rages in his too. We're two imperfect people, but together, we're something that defies description. Yin and yang. Light and dark. We're polarity, the force that balances all things.

Maybe I'm supposed to be a frightened, quivering little virgin. But I'm not. In his arms, I'm powerful and safe. His darkness calls to the sexual, curious woman inside, the one eager to explore all those fantasies that make me ache with longing.

I want to yield to this man, give myself over to him, but I don't trust easily. He wants to possess me, to ruin me for anyone else, but this complicated man wants to worship me too. This—the way I fight him, the way he revels in it—isn't about consent. It's about submission.

He wants to *earn* the right to claim me. And I need him to earn it too.

His arms lash around me, dragging me up his body. "Get your legs around my waist," he growls, his voice throbbing with dark urgency.

I hurry to obey this order, scrambling to lock them around his hips as he drags us from the sofa. As soon as we're up, he storms toward the house like the hounds of hell are nipping at his heels. We turn the corner as he jerks my skirt down, covering my ass.

"Keep everyone off the second floor," he snaps.

"Yes sir," Carmine says.

I frown, turning my head. Carmine stands beside Domani instead of Coda. He's staring straight ahead, not looking at me. And yet, I feel like he's staring directly at me.

"I'm not to be disturbed."

"Yes sir," Carmine says again.

Satisfied that his orders will be carried out, Rafe ducks inside the house, Carmine and Domani already forgotten.

"Where's Coda?"

"Busy," he grunts. "Get your teeth back in my skin, Amalia."

I thread my fingers through his hair, pulling his head back just hard enough to make it sting. "Feeling bossy, are we?" I ask when his eyes meet mine. "I already told you that I don't take orders from you."

His eyes blaze hot enough to rival the sun. "You'll take plenty of them when you're bouncing on my cock,

Amalia. You'll be a good little girl and do exactly what your king says."

My clit throbs at his promise.

"We'll see," I sniff, refusing to bend. "Maybe I'll give the orders. Maybe I won't bounce on your cock at all."

His eyes narrow to slits, a warning growl vibrating in his chest. Oh, he does not like to be told no. He turns for the stairs, taking them two at a time.

"Oh," I moan, locking my legs tighter around him as every step causes his erection to grind against my clit.

"That's what I thought," he says. "Don't fuck with me, Amalia. We both know you're dying to feel me wrecking that tight little cunt. It's all you've been thinking about since the first time I kissed you, isn't it?"

"N-no," I lie.

"Did you touch yourself in our bed while I was gone, *tesoro*?" he asks. "Did you bury your face in my pillow and pretend it was my hand between your legs?"

We reach the top of the stairs, my head lolling on my shoulders. I should be fighting him and defying him, but I can't. I'll do it in a minute. After I regroup.

"I thought about you," he says, setting off down the hall at a brisk walk. It's as if he doesn't even notice my extra weight. "Every fucking night I was gone, I thought about you alone in our bed, touching yourself, calling out my name. It nearly drove me mad. But I didn't give in. I didn't allow myself the pleasure."

The way he says it sets off an alarm in the back of my mind.

"Why did you leave?" I ask once we cross into the bedroom and the door closes behind us.

"I didn't trust myself to stay." He meets my gaze, still holding me in his arms. "I didn't deserve to stay. I could have hurt you. *Killed* you. When I realized I had you pinned beneath me..." Shame sears his expression. "I didn't bring you here to hurt you, Amalia."

"Why..." I lick my lips, terrified of his answer. "Why did you bring me here?"

"Because I had to."

My heart trembles, threatening to crack. "Because of Diego."

"No." His denial is soft, emphatic. "Women are off-limits under my rules, *tesoro*. Anyone who targets a woman faces death. I broke my own law for *you*, not for Diego. Because I took one look at you and knew you were mine."

"Rafe," I whisper, pretty sure he means it.

"You're mine, *tesoro*."

"I'm not yours," I say, plunging my hands into his hair to pull his head back. His gaze tangles with mine, all pissed off, territorial male. "Not yet, Rafe."

"Careful, little girl," he growls, his eyes heating like metal at a forge. "I've been dying to fuck the fight out of you since I met you. Don't tempt a desperate man."

Except that's exactly what I want to do. Tempt him. Rattle him. *Break* him. I want him desperate. Maybe I shouldn't like playing with fire, but I love the way this man burns.

"Then do it, Rafe," I say, commanding him this time. Ordering him. "Fuck me. Break me. *Claim* me."

I don't think either of us will be satisfied until he does. I need his stamp of ownership on me just as badly as he needs it. I need this part of me to belong to him and no other.

He growls my name, his hands flexing on my ass. His fingers dig into my cheeks and then relax. Dig in and then relax.

I lean forward slowly, my eyes locked on his. I hold his gaze until the last possible second and then bite his lip. Hard.

He roars in pleasure.

I land on my stomach on the bed, crying out his name. Within seconds he's on top of me, my skirt around my waist.

His hand comes down on my right cheek in a hard smack. The sharp sting sends a blast of pleasure through me.

"*Tigrotta*," he growls.

"Did you just *spank* me?"

He smacks my left cheek in response.

I bite my tongue, battling back a cry of ecstasy. Pissed that I love it, and thrilled that I do all at once.

"Don't pretend you don't fucking love it," he growls in my ear, nipping at the lobe. "I can smell how wet you are for me right now, Amalia."

"*¡Vete al demonio!*"

He laughs, the dark sound grating against my womb. "Nah, *tesoro*. I've been there. Tonight, I'm riding your curvy little body straight to heaven." His hand comes down on my ass again. "Don't worry though. You're going to love every minute of the ride."

I'm pretty sure he's right. Already, my body feels like it's on fire. My clit pulses. My nipples ache. I'm desperate for him to spank me again and outraged at the thought at the same time.

What is he doing to me?

He thrusts one hand between my legs, cupping my center through my panties. I moan in ecstasy, sobbing like the desperate, needy girl he's turning me into.

"Ride my hand, Amalia. Pump your hips and give me a show while I teach you how much you like to obey orders."

"*Rotto nel culo,*" I curse, fighting him even as I do exactly as he demands and grind against his hand. I can't help it. Part of me loves fighting him. The other part desperately wants to please him. I'm addicted to this man and the way he makes me feel. In his arms, I'm alive in a way I've never been. I'm more myself than I've ever been. I'm supposed to be his prisoner, yet I feel free for the first time in my life.

He delivers a sharp spank to my right cheek and then soothes it with his palm. I cry out, bucking against his hand, chasing the pleasure.

"That's it, *tesoro,*" he croons. "Use me as your own personal fuck toy. Make a mess for me to clean up."

*Oh, God.*

He smacks my left cheek.

My inner muscles clench.

He yanks the back of my panties down without warning, exposing my ass.

"Goddamn," he breathes. "You look good with my handprints painted across your skin, *tesoro*. I wish you could see how beautiful you look right now."

The reverence in his voice sends me over the edge. I

cry out his name and crash headlong into an orgasm. My nipples drag across the bed as I writhe and moan. And then I feel his lips on my ass where his handprints are...and get dragged under a brand-new wave.

I fall limp beneath it, letting it toss me about like a ragdoll.

Rafe rolls me over, brushing tendrils of hair gently out of my face.

"*Bellissima*," he murmurs, leaning down to kiss me gently. His tongue twines around mine, his kiss slow and sensual, erotic. It's like he's making love to my mouth. He runs his hands up and down my sides in languid strokes. Instead of bringing me back down to earth, he lifts me higher, leaving me floating five feet off the ground.

"Rafe," I moan, shifting restlessly beneath him. Unsure what I need. I just know I need more. "Please."

"You sound so sweet when you beg, *tesoro*," he murmurs against my lips. "Do you want to come again?"

"Please."

He breaks our kiss, gently sitting me up. Somehow, he manages to undress me with no help from me. I'm boneless, useless. He doesn't seem to mind. He croons praises in my ear, runs his hands across my body, constantly lifting me higher, higher, until I feel drugged with pleasure, drugged by him. Fighting him doesn't even cross my mind. I don't want to fight him.

He hasn't even gotten inside of me, and he's already stripped me of my defenses and ruined me. I'm in serious trouble here. I think he knows it too. I think he loves it. The cocky bastard loves every minute of this.

"Your turn," I say when I'm stripped bare, wearing nothing but a blush.

He smirks at me. "You want me naked, *tesoro*?"

I nod decisively.

He grins and rises from the bed like a graceful panther, all sleek and confident. Sure of himself. He strips without shame or reservation, leaving his suit draped over the bench at the foot of his massive bed. With clothes on, he's beautiful. Without them, he's breathtaking.

His body is a work of art. He's not ripped like a bodybuilder but made of thick muscle like a man approaching his forties. His abdomen isn't defined, but instead one hard slab. The mass of puckered flesh shatters pieces of my heart. It stands in testament to his strength, to his resilience.

"*Bellissima*," I whisper, lifting my gaze to his. I mean it. He is beautiful.

He prowls toward me, heat in his gaze. Pride. His erection bobs, jutting hard and proud from his body. He's big...bigger than I'm prepared to think about right now. But I want this. I want him. And I know he won't hurt me. I think this man would open a vein and bleed for me if I asked it of him. He's as caught in the maelstrom as I am, as incapable of walking away as I am. Whatever this is between us, he's all in too. I see it in his eyes, feel it in his touch. Even if it leaves us wrecked and ruined, he's all in.

He crawls onto the bed with me, capturing my lips

in another heated kiss. Before I can wrap my arm around his neck, he prowls down my body, leaving a trail of fire in his wake. His lips touch every inch of skin, explore every sensitive place on my body. He wrecks me with his lips and tongue, leaving me gasping.

"Rafe!" I cry out, clutching fistfuls of his hair when he sinks his teeth into the side of my breast, marking me. I leave claw marks down his back when he moves to my nipples, tormenting them with pleasure. He bites and sucks and licks. And then does it all over again.

I find my fight again. I bite him. Scratch him. Curse him. He laughs...and makes his way down my body, torturing me with pleasure. It's too much and not enough. The bastard is enjoying my torment. His eyes shine with amusement, with desire. The more I fight, the more he likes it.

"Fight me now, *tesoro*," he dares me, throwing my legs over his shoulders.

I shatter apart as soon as his tongue touches my clit, exploding into a thousand tiny pieces. He doesn't stop. He holds me down beneath him and eats me like I'm a four-course meal and he's in no hurry. I scream and sob and buck and writhe, alternately grinding against his face and trying to climb off, unsure if I want more or want the heavenly torment to end.

Rafe refuses to let me go. He eats me from one orgasm to the next, his fingers and tongue in places they shouldn't be. And I love it. God help me, I love every filthy minute of it. I come a third time with his fingers in my ass and his tongue in my center, screaming his name.

"Please, please," I sob, pleading for mercy.

"Poor little *tigrotta*," he croons, crawling up my body. He comes down over me, gently nudging his way between my legs. "Have you had enough?"

"No," I gasp. Not yet. Not until he's inside me.

"*Piccola guerriera*," he says, raining kisses across my face. One hand runs down my side, startling me. "Shh, *tesoro*. I'm going to take care of you."

"Will it...will it hurt?" I ask, thinking about his size again, not entirely convinced he's going to fit without causing serious damage down there. I'm not naïve. I know how sex works. But I can't help but worry now that the moment has come. Losing your virginity is uncomfortable for a lot of women. People love to blame it on the partner, but sometimes, I think it just plain hurts. At least that seems to be the case for most of the girls I went to school with.

"It might," Rafe says, not lying to me. "But the pain won't last long, Amalia. I promise I'll be as gentle as I can be." He rests his forehead against mine, being far too sweet. "Give the pain to me if it helps, *tesoro*. Bite me. Claw me. I can take it."

"I can take it," I whisper.

"Are you sure?"

"Yes."

He chuckles. "I mean are you sure you want to do this, Amalia? You can so no. I won't force you. I won't try to change your mind. You don't owe this to me."

"Rafe? Shut up and make love to me."

"As you command," he breathes, notching his erection at my entrance.

"Wait."

He freezes.

"You're not wearing a condom."

He looks at me, something dark and possessive in his gaze. "You're mine, Amalia. I'm taking you bare. There is no one but you. There hasn't been anyone but you since before you were born. There won't ever be anyone but you."

"I could get pregnant," I whisper, my stomach quivering at the thought. Not in fear, not in revulsion, but in...excitement. God help me, but I *like* the thought of carrying this man's child.

"Good," he grunts, that possessive darkness growing. He dips his head, putting his lips next to my ear. "You think I wouldn't be happy to breed you here and now, *mi reinita*? You think I wouldn't want to bring your child into this world?" He laughs quietly. "Little girl, I'm fucking *dying* to plant my kid in you."

"Rafe," I moan.

"Be a good little queen and try not to scream too loud when I do it, Amalia," he says. "Don't make me kill every man in this house who hears you screaming for your king."

*Oh my God.*

I go limp beneath him, a mini-orgasm quaking through me.

He chuckles, a wicked, devilish sound that sets fire to my veins. And then I feel his teeth in my skin.

A moment later, he rocks his hips forward, pushing into me. I moan loudly, so turned on, I can't even think straight. He licks and kisses my neck, sending my thoughts scattering in every direction as the head of his cock slips inside.

It burns a little, but it doesn't hurt.

"Rafe," I moan.

He pushes forward again, slipping in another inch. The burn intensifies slightly. Mostly, I feel stretched and full...and a little bit wicked. He's been tormenting me for hours now, slowly driving me out of my mind. Now, it's my turn.

"You feel so good," I whisper, turning my face so my mouth is next to his ear. "You're inside me, Rafe. You have what no one else will ever have. I'm yours."

Rafe roars...and breaks. He snaps his hips forward, impaling me on him in one swift thrust. A flash of pain washes through me, there and gone so quickly I barely feel it. I know what it means though. I know what it signifies. He just broke my hymen. He really does have a piece of me now that no one else ever will. I belong to him in a way that nothing and no one can ever undo or erase—not time, not distance, not even death.

"Fuck," he curses, breathing raggedly. "Are you okay, *tesoro*?"

"Perfect," I whisper through tears. "I'm perfect, Rafe."

"You're crying."

"I'm happy," I say, staring up at him. "You make me happy."

The worry bleeds from his eyes, his expression softening. "I know the feeling, *tesoro*."

I think maybe he does. I think if anyone understands what it's like to live life in a cage, this man does.

His may be more luxurious than mine, but it's a cage, nonetheless. Neither of us have ever been free. Neither of us have ever known true happiness. We've both snatched fleeting moments from beneath the blades of the swords hanging over our heads, but they never lasted long. This moment though...this one has the makings of forever.

"Make love to me," I whisper, tilting my face up to his in a silent demand for kisses. "Make me yours."

"You're already mine."

"Then prove it. *Baciami.*" *Kiss me.*

He growls. And he kisses me. Until I'm breathless and dizzy and more in love with him than I was even five minutes ago. God, I love him. I'm not falling. I already hit the ground, face first. I'm madly, wildly, desperately in love with this beautiful, complicated man.

His hips roll against mine, sending ripples of pleasure through my body. I gasp in shock, in delight, in ecstasy.

"You like that, huh?" he asks, chuckling. And then he does it again. And again. He pushes into me and then slides back, impaling me on him over and over again, hitting spots inside that have stars bursting behind my eyelids.

I cry out his name loud and then louder, clutching him to me. The louder I get, the harder he takes me. The harder he takes me, the louder I get. It's as if we feed off one another, our lovemaking growing wilder, more frenzied. He flips me onto my stomach, lifting my hips into the air before slamming back inside me.

My nipples drag against the blankets with every deep thrust.

"Fuck," he growls. "Spread your cheeks apart with your hands, *tesoro*. Let me see that pretty pink hole."

I should be embarrassed or offended or...something. But I'm not. With him, I feel no shame. I do exactly what he demands, willingly, without question. And he loves it.

"God yeah," he groans, and I know he's staring, looking at me right *there* as he pounds into me. He's deeper this way, so deep he steals my breath with every thrust.

He confirms my suspicion a second later when he presses his thumb to that hole, playing with it. I think he's obsessed with it. He can't seem to stop touching it. Is that normal? I'm not sure. But...I don't hate it.

"This is going to be mine too, Amalia," he says. "As soon as you're pregnant, I'll be claiming it too."

My muscles clench around him at the thought.

"Dirty girl," he says with a chuckle, and I know he felt it. He swats my cheek. "Come on. Up on your knees."

He has to help me up. Somehow, he manages to stay inside me. He positions us with me on my knees in front of him, his chest against my back. One hand sweeps my hair out of the way. The other encircles my throat.

"Grind back against my lap," he says in my ear. "Fuck yourself on my cock while I watch, *tesoro*."

My gaze shifts to the closet doors. I moan at the sight of us, at the way he hovers over me, almost protectively, his hand wrapped around my throat. My hair is a wild tangle, my skin flushed and damp with sweat. His marks litter my skin. My claw marks are etched into his. We look...beautiful together. Erotic. Sensual. Like a work of art.

"Look how fucking good you look," he growls, slipping his free hand between my legs.

I cry out, slamming myself down on him faster, harder, my eyes locked on the sight of us in the mirror. I can't look away. My whole life, people have called me names because I'm a big girl. I never cared because they didn't matter. But right this moment, I've never felt *less* like those things than at any time in the past.

This man is one of the most beautiful people in the city...but I'm his equal in every way. We don't just look good together. We *are* good together. We fit like puzzle pieces locking together. He was made hard because I was made soft. I was made soft because he was made hard.

"Rafe," I moan, trying to tell him what I see, what I feel.

"I know, *tesoro*," he says. "I know."

I lose track of rational thought then, give myself over completely to the pleasure. I slam myself down on him, using him to get myself off, to get him off. I grind and moan, taking him deep only to lift up and do it again. He plays with my clit, his hand around my throat.

But it's not enough. I need more. I need...something.

"Rafe," I sob in frustration, not sure what I need.

He knows though. His hand tightens around my throat, his fingers gripping tight along the sides. He doesn't cut off my air supply, but almost instantly, my orgasm starts to build. I grind down on his lap harder, faster, clawing at his arms, my mouth open in soundless bliss.

"Come," he growls, his eyes locked on mine in the mirror.

As soon as he speaks the command, he relaxes his grip. The blood rushes back to my head, a sense of euphoria sweeping through me.

I explode apart so fast, the room goes black.

Rafe roars, flipping me over onto my back. He thrusts inside me again, fucking me hard enough to rattle the headboard. He moves without rhythm, pounding so deep I know I'll feel him tomorrow. And then he falls still with a groan of ecstasy that sets off another detonation in my womb. Warmth fills me as he spills inside me, filling me so full of him that he splashes out, making a mess of both of us.

It's the single greatest moment of my life. And the most terrifying. Because in that moment I realize two things. I can't live without him. And I might not have a choice.

## CHAPTER 7

"You okay, *tesoro*?" I ask, holding Amalia as close as I can get her. She's quiet in my arms, her body plastered to mine. I'm not sure what she's thinking, but she hasn't let me go once. I'm taking that as a good sign. She couldn't get rid of me now even if she tried. Hell, even before I made love to her, what's left of my soul was hers to claim.

She owns me, mind, body, and soul.

But being inside her.... Either God believes I'm worthy of redemption or he wants an eternity in hell to hurt as much as possible. Because that was as close to heaven as I've ever been. If she's not a sign of salvation... if I'm destined to an eternity in hell without her in punishment for my sins, it'll be the worst torment he could have engineered.

"Yeah," she says, her voice soft and sweet. "Just thinking."

I smile. Of course she's thinking. That brain of hers never stops. She's a little tiger cub, constantly testing her boundaries, endlessly curious about her surroundings. Not even when sated is she tame. "What are you thinking about, *tigrotta*?" I ask, running my hand down the curve of her hip. My dick twitches, already eager for another round. "How you'll try to run away tomorrow? If my hot pink walls will look better with glitter or no glitter? What new ways you can shock my men?"

"Diego's my foster brother," she whispers, shocking me this time. She hasn't spoken a single word about Diego Butera since I brought her here. I haven't asked her about him either. She vowed not to tell me about him, and I promised myself not to make her break that vow.

My hand falters on her hip.

"Alvise Butera adopted me when I was ten. After Alvise died, Diego raised me."

"*Tesoro,*" I murmur, distressed on her behalf. "You don't have to tell me this."

"I know. I just...I just wanted you to know who he is to me," she says, turning slightly so one mocha eye peeks up at me. "He's my family."

"You were in foster care?" I ask instead of telling her that Mattia and I already worked out her connection to Diego for ourselves.

She nods. "I grew up in a group home."

My heart clenches. "What happened to your family, *tesoro*?"

She hesitates for a moment, something shifting through her expression too quickly for me to read. "They died," she says, her voice remote. "In a fire."

"Jesus," I whisper, pulling her closer. For the first

time, I let myself consider exactly how much she stands to lose here. Diego is her brother, the only family she has left. If I kill him—*when* I kill him, I'll be taking the last of her family from her.

My stomach twists. No part of me finds pleasure in this thought. No part of me relishes it. If Diego's death hurts her...*mafankulo*. For the first time, I realize just how fucked this entire situation is. We're rats in a maze, and the walls are caving in on us.

I think she knows it too. Her arms tighten around me as if she intends to mold us into one being and keep the outside world from intruding. She's not ready to lose this either. The bond between us is strong, but new. This threatens to shatter it, to shatter *us*.

"I'm not going to let you two kill each other," she says, lifting up suddenly. Her eyes meet mine, filled with stubborn determination. "I'm going to find a way to stop this stupid war before it gets one of you killed, Rafe."

"Ah, *tesoro*," I whisper, pulling her down to rain kisses across her crown. I don't have the heart to tell her that I fear it's already far too late for that. If I allow Diego to live now, there will be no stopping a war with Genovese. He'll throw everything he has at me. And when he's done, others will try their luck too. They'll see my leniency toward Diego as weakness, and they'll come one by one to try to take my crown. The streets of Chicago will run red with blood, and it'll be on my hands...and on Diego's.

If it weren't for my brothers, I'd give the other families the fucking keys to the kingdom. I would have handed them over the day my father died and told them to have fun dismantling his empire brick by brick. But I won't lose my brothers, and I won't lose Amalia. Not now, not ever.

What does that leave?

There is no path forward that doesn't end in destruction. If I kill Diego, I lose Amalia. If I allow him to live, I risk her life and the lives of my brothers. I've always chafed under the bonds of this empire, but for the first time I truly fucking loathe it.

One way or another, it'll cost me what I can't afford to lose. It'll cost me *her*.

No. I don't care who I have to fight or kill or indebt myself to or pay off. For twenty years, I've given everything to this fucking kingdom. It took my mother. It cost me the respect of my twin. I gave up my freedom, my future, and blackened my soul to keep my word and keep my brothers safe. I've given up enough. I won't allow this fucking life to take her too.

"This isn't your fight, Amalia," I tell her, dragging her back down into the bed with me. "This is between me and Diego. We'll resolve it without involving you."

"I'm already involved, Rafe. I'm your prisoner."

"Queen," I growl. "You're my queen, *tesoro*."

"Dario Marchesi," she blurts.

I blink at her.

"Diego hates you because of Dario Marchesi," she says, her gaze shifting back and forth across my face, her teeth sunk firmly into her bottom lip.

I frown, trying to place the name. A vague memory floats up. He was a *soldato* with a penchant for beating on women. He hospitalized his *comare* fourteen, fifteen years ago. It wasn't the first time. But it was the last.

"What about him?" I ask, not sure how Diego knows about him.

"He was Diego's biological father," Amalia says, her voice soft.

"Alvise Butera was Diego's father."

"No," she says with a shake of her head, "he wasn't. Alvise married Diego's mom when Diego was just a baby, but Dario was his biological father. He was in prison for drug trafficking, so he agreed to let Alvise adopt Diego. He kept in touch with Diego once he was paroled." She gives me a sad frown. "Diego knows you killed him, Rafe."

*Mafankulo.* That's what this is about? A fucking vendetta over Dario Marchesi? My hand twitches with the desire to grab my phone to call Mattia and Luca to fill them in, but I resist the urge. I've had enough talk of Diego Butera tonight. So has Amalia.

This night shouldn't be shadowed by dark things. When she remembers this night, I want her to remember only how good it was, and how adored she felt. There will be no sadness, no worry. I won't allow it. She is mine to care for, and right now, I'm doing a terrible job of it. It's time to correct that.

I roll her to the side and slide out from beneath her, rising to my feet. Before she can ask what I'm doing, I scoop her up into my arms. "Enough of this, *tesoro*," I murmur, leaning down to press a hard kiss to her swollen lips. "No more talk of Diego in our bed."

"We're going to talk in the bathroom instead?" she

asks, her nose scrunching as I carry her toward the en suite bathroom.

"No, smart ass," I say, chuckling. "We're not going to talk about him at all."

"What are we going to do then?" she asks, her eyes heating.

"I'm going to clean you up and take care of you," I murmur, striding toward the massive, jetted tub, looking forward to this part. To pampering her and caring for her. I find myself...eager to meet her every need, to be the one she trusts with this part of her. Intimacy with her is nearly as intoxicating as sex. "And if you're a very, very good queen, perhaps I'll get you all dirty again in the process."

She smiles at me, twining her arms around my neck. "What if I want to be a naughty queen, Rafe? What do I get then?"

"Show me how naughty you can be, *tesoro*," I growl, setting her on the vanity as my blood flashes to steam, "and I'll show you exactly what you get then."

"I need you to do something for me today, *tesoro*," I murmur, planting kisses all over the back of Amalia's neck early the next morning in the kitchen.

"What?" she moans, her fork tapping against her plate, her eggs long forgotten.

"I need you to stay inside. No trying to run away." Until we know who is trying to get their hands on her, I don't want her sticking a toe outside without me and Mattia by her side. And we have shit to do today. Like find whoever the fuck is after my girl, figure out what the fuck to do with Diego, stop a war. Typical Tuesday bullshit.

"Are Coda and Domani already tired of chasing me?" she asks, a smile in her voice.

"*Tesoro*, they were tired of chasing you on day two." I run my lips up the tendon on the side of her neck, growling when her body goes limp and pliant in my arms. Fuck everyone and everything responsible for making us leave the bed this morning. She should still be naked and riding my cock.

I didn't want to let her leave the bed at all. She fell asleep in my arms last night. For the first time in decades, my dreams weren't filled with horrors. It was if the ghosts of my past dared not come too close to her light. Instead, I dreamed of her, of a future I stopped hoping for long, long ago. New seeds sprout now, fragile shoots already reaching bravely toward the sun.

"Carmine will be helping Domani keep you in line today," I murmur.

Her body stiffens. "Where's Coda?"

"Busy."

She drops her fork, spinning to face me. "You said that last night. Where is he, Rafe?"

"Careful, *mi reinita*," I murmur, fighting an irrational surge of jealousy at the sight of the worry etched across her face. "Coda is...a friend. It would bother me a great deal to end his life for touching what doesn't belong to him."

Her face blanches. "Y-you think I'm *sleeping* with Coda?" she splutters.

"No," I admit, reaching for her. The thought never crossed my mind.

She bats my hand away, glaring daggers at me.

"You, I trust implicitly," I say, explaining quietly before she stabs me with her fork. "But I'm a possessive, jealous asshole when it comes to you, *tesoro*. Leaving another man to guard you makes me irrationally, murderously jealous. Knowing they get to spend their days watching over you, making you laugh, seeing that smile, hearing that smart mouth..." I reach for her again, reeling her in before she can dodge me. "Seeing the way your little nipples harden when you're cold and your hips sway when you walk..." I press my mouth to her ear. "I want to kill every man who even *breathes* near you, Amalia. That's what you do to me. That's how crazy you make me. That's how much I adore you."

"Rafe," she gasps.

*"Te adoro, mi reinita."* I nip her ear. *"Te adoro."*

*I adore you, my little queen. I adore you.*

"Rafe," she whispers again.

"Every moment you spend in the presence of another man is one I spend writhing in jealousy. I'm obsessed with you, *tigrotta*."

"Me too," she says simply. I know she means it. She doesn't flee from my confessions or cower from them. She accepts each one calmly, bravely, and then gives me her own, whispering them sweetly into my skin. "I'm obsessed with you too, Rafe."

"Promise me you'll stay inside today."

*"Lo prometo,"* she agrees, whispering her promise in Spanish.

I press my lips to the pulse beneath her ear and then reluctantly pull back. "Finish your breakfast," I murmur, turning her gently back toward her eggs. "I'll be back as soon as I can."

"Wait." She grabs my hand.

I meet her gaze.

"You know I would never do anything like that... right?" she asks, nibbling on her bottom lip. "I mean with any of your men. Or any other man." Her cheeks pinken. "I mean I wouldn't ever act inappropriately or try to make you jealous on purpose. I just like Coda better than Carmine, that's all."

"Why? Has Carmine done something?" I ask, instantly suspicious.

"N-no, of course not," she says, shaking her head.

She's lying. Badly.

"Tell me," I growl.

"He hasn't done anything, Rafe," she says. "I just don't like him, okay?"

I narrow my eyes on her, which only elicits the same response from her.

"I'm allowed to not like people without a reason if I want to, Rafael Valentino!" she growls, popping her hands on her hips to scowl at me. "I don't take orders from you."

"Amalia, *tesoro*." I pinch the bridge of my nose, taking a deep breath. She's hiding something, but I don't have time to sort it out right now. When I get home tonight, we'll finish this conversation. And she will be telling me what the fuck Carmine did to upset her. If he was stupid enough to try to put his fucking hands on her, I'll kill him slowly.

I don't think that's the case though. Amalia's a tough girl. She wouldn't hesitate to rip his balls off and feed them to him if he crossed a line. She seems almost...panicked at the thought of me finding out what she's hiding. I doubt it's because she's trying to protect him. I'm guessing he caught her doing something she shouldn't be doing and she's either embarrassed about it or afraid I'll be pissed about it. She doesn't like him because he knows something she doesn't want him to know.

Whatever it is, I don't want to hear it from him. She'll be the one telling me what happened. And then I'll deal with him for keeping it from me. Later.

"We'll discuss this later," I murmur to Amalia. "I have to go."

"There's nothing to discuss," she sniffs, her chin thrusting stubbornly into the air.

I smile at the sight, my dick turning to steel in my slacks. Christ. Why does that attitude turn me on so fucking much? It's as sexy as it is cute. As soon as she gets feisty, I want nothing more than to toss her over my shoulder, carry her upstairs, and then fuck the attitude right out of her. And once she's blissed out and purring, I want to cuddle the fuck out of her.

I growl at the thought and stomp toward her, dragging her into my arms. She fights me until my mouth crashes down on hers, and then she goes pliant, melting like the sweetest little treat. A loud moan breaks from her lips, weakening my resolve. I devour her mouth, one hand clutched in her hair, the other gripping her round ass.

"Rafe," she moans.

"I like my name better when you're screaming it, Amalia," I mutter, biting her bottom lip. "Especially when you've got that juicy cunt wrapped around my cock and your claws in my back while you're screaming it."

She whimpers this time, trembling against me.

"Fuck," I groan, pressing my forehead to hers, breathing raggedly. My dick throbs, begging for relief. "You can't make that sound right now."

"Then stop saying dirty things to me!" she cries.

"Stop making it so fucking easy to say them to you."

"It's not my fault you have a dirty mouth."

"Ah, *tesoro*," I chuckle through a groan. "I didn't have a

dirty mouth until I met you. I was a cold, heartless bastard. Women didn't exist to me. You ruined me, Amalia. That fucking mouth. Those incredible breasts. Your goddamn thighs and that round ass." I smack her cheek to illustrate my point, growling when it bounces and jiggles. "Your bright eyes and wild spirit. Your gentle heart and fierce courage." I exhale a soft breath, shaking my head in disbelief that she's mine. *"Sei l'la donna dei miei sogni."*

*You're the woman of my dreams.*

"Rafe, I—"

"Boss."

Amalia freezes as soon as Domani's apologetic voice sounds behind me. Whatever she was about to say slips away, the moment gone. I groan, burying my face in her hair. I've never wanted to kill someone as badly as I want to kill Domani Brambilla in this moment.

"What?" I growl, pretty fucking certain he just ruined her telling me that she's in love with me. Suddenly, her dislike of Carmine doesn't seem so suspicious considering that I suddenly, and very greatly, dislike Domani.

"Luca's here," he says. "He says you two have a meeting in Whiting. He's waiting in the Bentayga."

"Shit. The board meeting."

"Board meeting?" Amalia pulls back to blink wide eyes at me.

"One of our companies," I mutter, glancing at my watch. The last thing I want to deal with right now is a board meeting. They piss me off on a good day. Today is not one of those. I don't have the patience nor the time.

"Oh. I forgot you're a fancy-pants businessman too."

Domani coughs into his hand to hide a smile.

"I'm a lot of things, *tesoro*. I don't think anyone would call me a fancy-pants businessman," I say, shaking my head at her. Fuck, she's cute.

"Oh, that's right," she says, snapping her fingers. "They prefer MILF."

"MILF?"

"Mmhmm," she hums, pure mischief in her mocha eyes. "I believe it stands for Mafioso I'd like to fu–"

I cut her off with my mouth on hers, swallowing her laughter.

"Dammit," I whisper, nudging the bottom drawer of Rafe's desk closed with my foot. For a mafia boss, his desk is ridiculously boring. And meticulously arranged. I take a moment to rearrange everything on top, smiling to myself. I bet it'll drive him nuts when he sees it. He probably has to have everything in a very specific order, or it throws his whole system off.

He's so...I'm not sure there is a word for him, honestly. He's a dichotomy of extremes. He's the sun, scorching hot, able to burn you to ash with a single glance. He's also the Boomerang Nebula, colder even than space, able to freeze you solid in a nanosecond. There's nothing simple about him. He's fierce. And beautiful. And kind. And affectionate. And a million wonderful things that make my heart race and my knees weak.

I never stood a chance against him. I'm so in love with him it's terrifying. Literally. I feel like we're

133

balancing on razor-wire. One wrong move, and we all fall down. How do I sacrifice Rafe to save Diego? How do I save Diego if it means sacrificing Rafe? I can't. I can't. Somehow, there has to be a way to nudge them off the tracks before they collide.

I pull open the top drawer of the desk and peek inside, hoping some solution might have magically appeared since I last looked. The contents of the drawer are as useless as they were three minutes ago.

"Looking for something?"

I startle in my chair, my gaze flying to the door. Carmine's leaning against the doorjamb, watching me with a smirk on his face. It seems calculated and sinister to me. He's been looking at me the same way all day. It's driving me nuts. It's like he knows something I don't.

I snuck into the office an hour ago to escape him in the first place. Rafe's been gone all day, and the longer Carmine stares at me, the more unsettled I feel. I tried to read but couldn't focus with his eyes on me, making my skin crawl. I tried watching television with the same results. I trooped up and down the stairs, exploring every room in the house.

"Yeah, the number to 911," I mutter sarcastically. "Do you happen to know it?"

"I'll make you a deal," he says, poking his head out into the hall. He glances both ways and then steps into Rafe's office with me, closing the door behind him. My heartbeat instantly goes into overdrive, warning bells sounding like gongs in my head. "You tell me what you're really looking for in his desk, and I won't tell him who you really are."

"Open the door," I say, my voice shaking. I slide Rafe's desk chair back, climbing to my feet. Instead of moving away from the desk, I stay close, ready to grab the letter opener in case I need a weapon. Whatever he's doing in here, well, I'm guessing he didn't come to chat over tea and cookies. He cornered me for a reason.

"I'm not going to hurt you, Serafina."

"That's not my name."

His smirk grows. "Are you sure about that?"

"My name is Amalia."

"Liar," he says, leaning back against the door, arms crossed over his chest. "I did some digging into you. Amalia Santiago didn't exist until the day Alvise Butera adopted you. I wasn't sure how that was possible, so I asked around. Name changes are part of the adoption process."

I swallow hard, my heart hammering.

"You could have gone with Butera, but you didn't. You picked your mom's name," he says, cocking his head to the side. "And her birthplace. Amalia Santiago. Your adoption records confirmed it. You're Serafina Cerrito."

He's not just guessing this time. He knows who I am. If he's seen the adoption records, he has proof. Those records were supposed to be sealed. No one was ever supposed to be able to find them. Alvise made sure of it.

How did Carmine get them? I don't think it matters at this point. However he got his hands on them, he knows what they contain. He'll tell Rafe.

Rafe. Oh my God.

The room spins. I grasp onto the desk, fighting for calm. Fighting for breath that won't come. What's Rafe going to say when he knows the truth? My insides shrivel at the thought. I love him. I didn't mean to fall for him, but I did. I can't lose him now. Not like this.

"What do you want?" I ask woodenly.

"You."

My stomach heaves, bile crawling up my throat.

"I'll kill us both before I let you touch me," I swear, meaning every word. There's no way in hell I'll let him touch me, not to keep my secret, not to save my life, not for any reason. My body is my own and I decide who to give it to. The thought of this man touching me like Rafe touches me, of this man's hands on me, his mouth on me... *Hell no.* I belong to one man, mind, body, and soul.

"Valentino may enjoy bedding *balenas*, but I'm not him. I have different tastes." His gaze flicks up and down my body. Despite his hateful words, I see the interest in his eyes, the curiosity. He's lying. Why? "I don't want to fuck you. I want you to leave with me."

"Why?"

"Because I'm not the only one who knows who you are," he says. "There's a price on your head. Millions. I intend to be the one to collect it."

I gape at him, pretty sure he's lost his mind. "They're not just going to let you walk out of here with me, Carmine!"

"I'm going to tell Domani that you ran," he says, speaking calmly. "He'll clear the house looking for you. When he does, we're leaving through the west wing.

You'll get in my car. You won't make a sound. You won't resist. You'll be a good little *principessa* and do what you're told."

I bristle, my hand twitching toward the letter opener. I'm not going with him. Rafe may hate me when he finds out the truth, but so long as I'm alive, there's a chance for me to fix it. There's still a chance for me to save both Rafe and Diego. If I leave with Carmine, we all suffer. We *all* die.

I may not know much about this world, but I know enough to know that's exactly how this particular story ends. There isn't a fairytale waiting on the other side of that car ride. There's pain and agony and death for me. There's the inevitable collision between Rafe and Diego. There's war. I can't find a way to stop that if I'm dead or in chains, sold to the highest bidder.

I can't run with Carmine blocking the door either. I need him to think I'm cooperating. Once we're out of the office, I'll make a run for it. Rafe will find out who I really am. He'll know that my father killed his mother and almost killed him. He'll know I lied.

*Forgive me, Rafe. Please, God, forgive me.*

"Fine," I growl to Carmine, my decision made. Even if it costs me Rafe. Even if it costs me everything. I'd rather him hate me and survive than love me and die. So long as he and Diego live, nothing else matters.

"Stay here," Carmine says, as if he knew I'd see it his way. His arrogance is as amusing as it is infuriating. He's playing a game he doesn't even understand. And for what? Money? No, that's not it. It's me. He wants to take me from Rafe, not because he wants me but because Rafe told him not to touch me. That's what this is about. He wants what doesn't belong to him simply because he was told he can't have it.

He's a gnat who thinks he's a giant. Rafe will kill him for this betrayal. He won't hesitate or blink. He won't even pause or ask questions. As soon as he finds out what Carmine did, he'll kill him. There will be no explanations or pardons. Carmine's story will end in a shallow grave, his name forgotten before the dirt even levels.

As soon as his back is turned, I grab the letter opener off the desk, shoving it into the pocket of my skirt. I bite my lip, holding back a sob of relief that this skirt actually has pockets. When this is over, I'm writing a thank you letter to the designer.

Carmine pulls the door open, sticking his head out into the hallway. "Domani!" he shouts. "She slipped out a window. Headed across the east lawn!"

A clatter sounds as the house clears, everyone inside immediately taking off to find me. It would be funny if it weren't so damn terrifying. And it's entirely my fault. They believe him because I've done nothing but try to run away since Rafe brought me here. They've been chasing me for days now, only for me to let myself be cornered or outran or outsmarted and silently marched back inside. Time and time again.

"Let's go," Carmine orders.

I stomp toward him, glaring daggers. "Rafe is going to kill you when he finds out you're the one who took me," I say, finding immense satisfaction in that fact. I shouldn't...but I do. I don't think I've ever truly hated anyone until this moment. But I hate this man. It burns like acid in my stomach, hardening my spine, turning my resolve to steel.

Carmine grabs my arm hard.

"Let me go."

"Start walking, *principessa.*"

I press my free hand against my side, feeling for the letter opener. The weight of it steadies me, gives me courage. I take a breath. And take a step.

Carmine stays right beside me, his fingers digging into my flesh hard enough to bruise. I hope Rafe makes him pay for every single one of them. We move swiftly toward the foyer. I decide to make my move there. It's the best place, the only logical place.

Moving carefully, I slip the letter opener out of my pocket, hiding it in my fist. My knees shake so hard I'm terrified my legs are going to give out beneath me. I've never been this scared before in my life. Not even when Rafe's men showed up on my doorstep.

*Rafe, I love you. I love you so much.*

As soon as we step over the threshold from the hallway into the foyer, I swing the letter opener toward Carmine's thigh with as much force as I can. For a split second, the metal fails to penetrate.

A voice in my head wails in fury.

And then the dull edge rips through his flesh, sinking deep.

"*Figlio di puttana!*" he roars, flinging me away from him with his hand on my arm.

I scream as my feet come out from beneath me and I go flying across the room, the letter opener still clutched in my hands. I feel it ripping free of his flesh. Hear his howl of pain as it does. I land against the wall closest to the stairs so hard it knocks the breath out of me.

Before I can catch my breath, let alone think about getting up and running, Carmine spins on me, rage on his face. His pants are ripped, blood pouring from the wound on his leg. It soaks into the dark fabric, spreading rapidly. Spots drip onto the tiles, leaving a trail of blood as he limps toward me.

I raise my hands up to fend him off...and then he's gone. Plucked from the ground like a ragdoll. Rafe lifts him completely off his feet and flings him across the room, roaring like an enraged bear. Hellfire burns in his chocolate eyes, searing his expression with pure murder. His jaw is rock hard, every muscle in his body taut.

Carmine's body slams into the credenza table. The table crumples beneath his weight, crashing to the floor with him on top of it. He doesn't move again.

For a long moment, silence reigns in the room. It's deafening.

"Get him the fuck out of here," Rafe snarls to Domani. "And bandage his leg. I want him alive when I get to him."

"Got it," Domani says.

I watch in silence as Domani and Vito haul Carmine up from the wreckage. They aren't careful about it. His head bangs against the wall as Domani hefts him over his shoulder. He hangs limp and unmoving.

My stomach twists.

I quickly avert my gaze, only for it to land on the blood smeared across the floor. Carmine knows who I am. He just tried to kidnap me. Because someone else knows too. Someone out there is offering millions to get their hands on me.

"Amalia."

I flinch, cowering against the wall as Rafe squats in front of me.

"It's me, *tesoro*," he says, his voice soft. "It's just me."

I stare at him, unable to tear my gaze away. Unable to think straight.

"Can you put down the letter opener, *tesoro*?" he asks. "I swear, I'm not going to hurt you."

I glance from him to my hands, only to realize he's right. I'm still clutching the letter opener in my hands. Carmine's blood still drips from the end of it. I cry out and fling it away from me, shuddering in revulsion.

I just stabbed a man.

"Rafe," I sob as the dam bursts.

He pulls me into his arms, wrapping himself around me. "Shh, *tesoro*," he breathes, holding me like he doesn't intend on ever letting me go again. "Shh, *amore mio. Sono qui ora. Sono qui.*"

"Has he said anything?" I ask Mattia, slipping into the warehouse at the harbor where he's holding Carmine. It's late and I'm fucking exhausted, but I won't sleep until this motherfucker is dead. He put his hands on Amalia, tried to take her from me. The only reason he's alive right now is because she needed me.

She's been inconsolable. Every tear she shed burned like acid. The monster inside howled in fury over each and every one, demanding blood, screaming for vengeance. I want to kill him slowly, painfully, make him pay for every second of fear and grief she's endured today. I also desperately want to get back to her. The devil wars with the lover, and I'm not sure which side is winning right now. It's a hell of a thing, realizing both sides are in perfect accord on one subject only. Her.

Everything I do now is for her.

"Some," Mattia says, his expression grim. His

knuckles are bruised, the cuffs of his shirt stained with Carmine's blood. "You aren't going to like it."

"Tell me."

"He's working for Genovese."

"*Mafankulo,*" I growl.

"Genovese wants the girl. He thinks she's someone else."

"Who?"

"Carmine won't say."

"Won't say or doesn't know?"

"Won't say." Mattia gives me a look. "Whoever Genovese thinks she is, he doesn't want you to know. I've worked this *testa di cazzo* over and he's not talking. I can try again but..." He glances over his shoulder at Carmine.

I follow his gaze. Carmine is pale, blood dripping from multiple cuts on his face. His shirt is soaked with it. So are his pants. And still, he sits upright, his head held high, a smirk on his face. He won't break. He's Cosa Nostra. We don't bow. We don't bend. We certainly don't fucking break. We're tempered steel, forged in the fires of *Omertà*. Silence is encoded in our DNA. It's who we are.

Who the fuck do they think Amalia is? And why are they so desperate to keep me from finding out? I don't know, but I don't like it. Better question. Why the fuck did Genovese warn me about the price on her head if he was the one who set it?

"Let me see your knife," I say, holding out my hand to Mattia.

He hands it over without question.

I pace toward Carmine who watches me with that same smirk. I see the wariness in his eyes though, the pain and the exhaustion. He's not nearly as unaffected as he'd like us to think. He'll keep his mouth shut until the very end because that's who he is, but it'll cost him.

"I warned you about touching her," I say quietly, fighting the urge to sink the knife into him. As much as I want to do it, as much as I want to make him pay over and over again for touching her...there's more at stake here than satisfying my own perverse need to make this motherfucker suffer until the very end. "Now you have a choice to make."

"What choice?"

"You can answer my questions and I'll kill you quick," I say. "Or you can piss me off and I'll do exactly what I said I would. I'll kill you so fucking slowly you'll howl for death by the time I'm done." I smile, a cold, deadly smile. "Your choice, Carmine."

"I'm not telling you who she is."

"That's not one of my questions."

He eyes me warily.

"Why did Genovese warn me about the bounty on her?"

"He knew chasing the lead would keep you busy and give me time to get her out of there," he says a little too quickly. He's lying. I'm just not sure why.

"If he's so interested in her, why didn't he grab her before I brought her home with me?"

"I can't answer that."

"Can't or won't?"

"Won't."

Which is answer enough, I suppose. Either he didn't know about her before I brought her home with me, or he wants her out of my hold specifically. Or both. If I had to guess, I'd say he didn't know about her until she was under my roof...and he requested the sit-down to find out how much I knew about her. He doesn't want me to know who she is and he's praying I don't find out before he gets his hands on her.

So who the fuck does he think she is?

I'm too goddamn tired to even try to figure it out tonight.

I circle around behind Carmine's chair and cut the tape binding his hands, ready to get this over with so I can get home to Amalia. Right now, more than anything, I just want to hold her in my arms and remind myself that she's okay. This motherfucker didn't get out of the house with her. Genovese didn't get his hands on her. She's safe in our bed where she belongs. No one took her from me. And no one will. Whoever they think she is, whatever game they're playing, they won't win. She's mine, today, tomorrow, always.

"Get up," I growl.

Carmine doesn't argue. He doesn't fight. He hauls himself to his feet, not speaking. We file out of the warehouse with Mattia following behind us. The wind blowing in from the lake is frigid, whipping the bottom of my jacket around.

"Stop," I order Carmine once we reach the edge of the dock. The board would have a communal fit if they knew I'd be dumping a body off the same dock we argued about not even twelve hours ago. They'd keel over if they knew just how many times this same scene had played out here over the years.

Mattia stands back, obscured in shadows. He doesn't speak. He merely observes quietly, ready to intervene if Carmine tries anything stupid. He doesn't. He's Mafioso to the end. Defiant. Proud. Unyielding. He tells me to go fuck myself. I tell him that he never should have touched what didn't belong to him.

He cracks when I raise the gun. Fear lights his eyes for the first time all night.

I find no satisfaction in it. And that's the moment I realize that loving Amalia has already changed me in ways so profound, I never even noticed until just this second. I don't relish this moment. I'm not amused. I'm not ferociously angry. I'm just...really fucking worried about Amalia. She's all I'm thinking about. She's all I'm ever thinking about.

Until I pull the trigger.

A scream rips apart the night, startling me. Before Carmine's body even falls into the water, I spin toward the sound, my eyes locking on a curvy blonde hiding between two barrels of oil on the far side of the dock. Her eyes are wide and stricken in her pale face, her mouth still open on her now soundless scream. She's tiny, barely even five foot tall. And she definitely shouldn't be here.

How the fuck did she even get in? This is restricted property.

"Fuck," I growl, taking a step toward her.

She snaps her mouth closed and takes off running.

I tip my head back and growl a string of curses up at the sky.

"I've got her," Mattia says, already running after her.

I leave him to it, knowing he'll catch her long before I do. Jesus Christ. Where did she come from? The situation isn't even remotely funny, but a burst of laughter escapes my lips anyway. Considering that I have no lawyer, the last thing I need is to be hauled in on a murder charge right now. Actually, in the grand scheme of things, being hauled in on a murder charge right now would be the least of my worries.

I dump the ammo from the gun, and then remove the slide and firing pin, tucking them into my pocket to dispose of elsewhere. Once that's done, I toss the rest of the gun far into the lake. Carmine's already sinking beneath the water. Within minutes, he'll be under. Eventually, he'll wash up somewhere.

If Mattia finds our witness, Chicago PD will rattle cages and make noise like usual. And then they'll add Carmine's case to the hundreds of other unsolved homicides stacking up on their desks. If Mattia doesn't find our witness...well, it's a good thing I have a house full of men prepared to swear that I've been home all night.

I turn my back on the lake to wait for Mattia.

Five minutes later, he comes jogging back down the dock.

"She slipped away," he mutters.

"*Figlio di puttana!*"

"She dropped her phone." He holds it up for me to see. "Ricci will have it cracked within the hour."

"I may be in handcuffs by then," I mutter.

"She committed at least half a dozen felonies breaking into this property," he says with a snort. "We'll find her long before she works up the nerve to go anywhere near a police station. Here." He tosses me the phone. "Take it to Ricci. You were never here."

"I need you to figure out what the fuck is going on."

"I know," he says, blowing out a breath. "You don't even have to say it."

"I'm going to say it anyway. He tried to kidnap her."

His jaw hardens. "*Stronzo.*"

He's worse than that. Genovese too. The motherfucker sat across from me and told me that his wife sleeps at night because of me. And then he sent Carmine into my home to kidnap my girl. Diego may have started this war, but I'm going to end it. Genovese is going to die by my hand for sending Carmine after Amalia. I'll take out his entire fucking family too if they get in my way.

"I want to know what they know," I growl. "And then I'm going to kill Genovese."

Mattia smiles, a vicious, deadly smile. "I'll help."

"**Y**ou're not going to like this," Ricci says two hours later.

"Are you guys reading from a fucking script today?" I ask, eyeing him over the rim of my glass of brandy. He's the second—or maybe the third—person who has said that to me today. Frankly, I'm tired of hearing it. Especially since they're right every single time. Whatever they say next is something I don't like.

"Sir?"

"Just tell me."

"Her name is Norah Bishop," he says. "She's, ah, an astrophysics student at Northwestern."

"You're fucking kidding me."

He shakes his head.

"Nico?" I ask.

He nods once.

I drain my glass.

"The universe is fucking with me," I mutter. There's no other explanation. God finally had enough of my bullshit. He's going to make me pay for every single one of my sins. Not one at a time, not little by little, but all at once. When I fall from my perch, he intends to leave a crater in my wake, a reminder for anyone who thinks to follow in my footsteps.

Fine. If he wants me to pay, I'll pay. But I'm doing it my way.

"Find her," I growl, dropping my glass on the table.

"Yes, sir."

"And Ricci? If you harm a single hair on her head, I will lose my goddamn mind," I say before stomping from the room.

Jesus Christ, fuck this whole day.

"Rafe?" Amalia whispers when I step out of the bathroom.

"Yeah, *amore mio*. It's me." My heart bleeds at the sight of her curled up in a ball in our bed. She looks so fucking small, so fragile. She's larger than life to me, a queen among women. It kills me that

Carmine stole even a fraction of that confidence and fire from her.

I cross to her, sliding into the bed behind her.

She trembles in my arms like she's cold.

"*Sono qui,*" I whisper in her ear, pulling her close.

"Is...is it done?"

I hesitate and then sigh. "It's done, *tesoro.*"

"Is it wrong that I'm glad?"

I gently flip her onto her back, brushing her hair from her face. Faint light spills into the room from the bathroom, allowing me to see her. She's so beautiful. God. Even with tears staining her face, she's ravishing.

"You're allowed to feel relief that the man who hurt you is gone, Amalia," I say, my voice firm. "You're allowed to be glad that he's dead. You aren't a monster for being human, *amore mio.*"

"Rafe," she whimpers, tears welling in her eyes.

"You're safe now." I run my thumbs beneath her eyes, brushing away her tears. And then I replace them with my lips, raining kisses across her face. "You're safe, Amalia."

"I was so scared," she whispers. "I k-knew if I l-let him get me out of t-the house, I'd d-d–"

"Shh, *tesoro. Sono qui.* He'll never get you out of this house. He'll never touch you. He'll never hurt you. No one will. You're mine to protect now. *Sei la mia vita. Ti amo,*" I whisper in Italian, and then in English. "You're my life. I love you, Amalia."

"Rafe," she sobs. "*Te amo. Te amo. Te amo.*"

For twenty-seven years, shards of ice have caged my heart, growing out of control. The day I met her, they finally began to thaw. I felt my heart beat again. Her confession shatters every fragment of ice still clinging, obliterating it. My heart doesn't just beat. It pounds, thundering against my ribcage until I feel dizzy with life. With love, as if it alone fuels me, coursing through my veins.

"Amalia," I rasp, seeking her mouth with mine. I pour my soul into her, letting her mend and heal it, letting her claim it.

She does, snatching it back from hell with the sweetest battle cry. It's my name, whispered from her lips. She clings to me, pulling me closer, as if she intends to drown herself in me. I let her. When she rolls us, I let her do that too. I'm hers to command.

She straddles my hips, stretching eagerly toward my mouth. Her sweet center nestles against my cock. I want to be a gentleman and simply kiss her. But my dick is a bastard. He roars to life, reaching toward heaven. She's naked and he's desperate. Always so desperate when it comes to her.

She moans, grinding against me.

"Amalia, *amore mio*," I groan, planting my hands on her hips. "Not tonight. Not after today. You need time."

"I need *you*!" she cries. "Please, Rafe. *Ho bisogno di te.*"

I don't deny her again. I can't. Whatever she needs, whatever she wants is hers.

"I'm yours, *amore mio*," I groan. "Take me."

She lifts up, notching me at her entrance. We cry out together when she sinks down on me, taking me to the hilt in one deep thrust. Ah, God. She's everything. *Everything.*

I drag her down to me, seaming our mouths together. She rolls her hips, taking me deep again and again. We get lost in one another. I get lost in her. Falling deeper, deeper.

Fuck, how did I ever live without her? How did I survive in a world without her light? Without her touch? I don't know. But I never will again. She's mine now, and I won't let her go. Not for Genovese. Not for Diego. Not for anyone.

"Rafe," she gasps, writhing on top of me as her orgasm begins to wash over her. "You f-feel s-so good."

"That's because I was made for you." I grip her hips, grinding her down on me, wanting her to take every ounce of pleasure she can get from me. "I was put on this earth to be yours, Amalia. You own me. You'll always own me. *Te amo*, my queen."

"Rafe!" She comes with a sharp cry of ecstasy, her nails embedded in my shoulders, her thighs cinched tight around my hips. Her pussy locks down around my cock, milking my shaft.

I yank her down on me as I come too, a choked sob of bliss leaving my lips. Goddamn. She's beautiful. So fucking beautiful. If this is atonement, I'll gladly pay. For however long I have to pay. Whatever price I have to pay. Whatever it takes to keep her with me.

She slumps forward on my chest, breathing hard.

"I love you," I whisper in her ear.

"Rafe," she whispers back.

## CHAPTER 10

*Amalia*

"What are you doing?"

"Ahh!" I scream, jumping a foot into the air. I whirl around to find Rafe standing behind me, glowering like I just tried to set his bed on fire. "You scared the crap out of me. Stop sneaking up on me!"

"I didn't sneak, Amalia."

"You're a freaking ninja."

"You're avoiding the question."

"I'm trying to look outside."

"Absolutely not."

I throw my hands up in the air, caught between the desire to scream and the desire to cry. It's been three days since Carmine tried to kidnap me, and Rafe has lost his mind. I thought having Coda and Domani following me around was bad. I was wrong. Having Rafe following every step I make is infinitely worse. When he doesn't like what I'm doing, he just picks me up and moves me. And he rarely likes what I'm doing.

Too close to the windows? Nope.

Doors? Forget about it.

Balconies? Ha!

I haven't seen outside in three days. It's driving me nuts.

I love him for being worried about me, but this is overkill. No one is going to kidnap me if I walk by a window. Nothing is going to happen to me if I crack open the kitchen door and peek outside.

Try telling him that.

He knows someone is after me. He just doesn't know why. For some reason, Carmine didn't tell him. A thousand times, I've opened my mouth to confess everything...only for words to fail me. I'm terrified he's going to hate me. I've been lying to him since the beginning. About who I am. About what I intended to do here.

He deserves the truth. I *know* he does. But I can't find the words to give it to him.

How do I tell him when I know it's going to break his heart? When I know he's going to hate me? I just found him. I'm selfish and horrible for wanting to keep him, and I know that, but I *do* want to keep him. So damn badly.

I need to talk to Diego. I need to tell him that I quit. That I'm not going to help him bring Rafe down and that everything has changed...except I have no way to make that call.

"You're not going outside, Amalia," Rafe says, pacing toward me. "It's too dangerous."

"Rafe." I take a deep breath. "Nothing is going to

happen if I open the door to let a little fresh air in. I haven't seen the sky in three days. I'm going stir crazy. I won't even stick a toe outside. I just want to *see* the world outside this house."

He eyes me doubtfully.

"Please," I plead. "I'll be good. *Lo prometo.*"

"*Cazzo!*" he growls, stomping toward the door. He flings it open, muttering under his breath the whole time. He's tense, his jaw clenched so hard it's in danger of cracking.

Guilt whispers through me. He's not being crazy for the fun of it. He's genuinely worried about me. Three days ago, someone he trusted tried to kidnap me. His enemy is offering millions for me to be brought to him. And he doesn't know why.

"Thank you," I say, reaching for his hand.

"I can't ever tell you no," he mutters, slipping his hand into mine. He pulls me toward him, wrapping his arms around me.

"Because you love me." I cuddle up against his chest, letting him hold me.

"I do love you." His lips touch my crown, lingering there.

Guilt threatens to crush me.

*Tell him. Tell him!*

"Rafe, I know wh–"

"Boss."

We both turn to look at Domani, who stands just inside the kitchen, his broad shoulders filling the doorframe. I swear, none of these guys ever missed a meal. It's like they all went to bodyguard school.

Huh. Maybe they did. Or the Mafia equivalent anyway.

"Mattia says your brother is here," he says, his expression grim.

Rafe tenses.

"Luca?" I ask, frowning. He stops by a lot. I haven't met Gabe yet, but I know Rafe sees him often too. Well, under normal circumstances he does. These are anything but normal circumstances. Rafe hasn't left the house at all since the night he...dealt with Carmine.

"Dr. Valentino," Domani says.

"Dr Valentino?" I repeat, and then realization dawns. "Nico? Nico is here?"

Domani nods.

"Amalia, *amore mio*, wait for me in the library," Rafe says.

I gape at him.

He's tense, lines of worry etched into his face. He looks older than he did a week ago, as if he's aged a decade in the last eight days. I know I should listen for once and go wait in the library. But everyone else in his life jumps when he says jump. They do exactly what he tells them to do when he tells them to do it. No one fights for him or what he needs or what's best for him. They do what they're told like good little soldiers.

I'm not a soldier. And I've never been very good at taking orders. But I know this man. I know his heart. And I know it's been bleeding for twenty years because of the rift between him and his twin. He misses Nico intensely. It's a phantom pain, one that never diminishes or goes away. They shared everything for eighteen years, a bond closer than brotherhood. If I can help bring them back together, I have to try.

"No," I say, pulling out of his arms.

He reaches for me, but I dart away, already running toward the dining room.

Rafe curses behind me, and then I hear him and Domani coming after me.

"Amalia, *tesoro*, I'm going to spank your pretty little ass if you step outside," Rafe growls behind me. "It's not safe for you."

"He's an astrophysicist, not the bogeyman, Rafe. If you aren't going to find a way to bring him back into this family, then I will!" I call over my shoulder, racing toward the front door. I don't think he's trying very hard to catch me. He could have by now if he really wanted to do it. I'm not fast.

"Amalia," he growls. "Get back here before I tie you to the bed!"

Oh, he's lost his mind if he thinks he's tying me to the bed.

"You are not tying me to the bed!" I yell, flinging the front door open and then marching down the stairs. I see Nico's car in the driveway, but I ignore it, spinning to face Rafe, who marches out behind me.

Is he *smiling?*

*"No recibo órdenes tuyas. ¡Tú y tus reglas pueden irse al infierno, Rafael Valentino!"* I growl, my hands on my hips.

He stares at me for a moment, his expression soft, making it hard to be mad at him. And then his gaze drifts from me to his twin. His smile slips, his expression going carefully blank. But not before I see the flash of pain in his eyes. It's the same ancient grief that marked him when he spoke of Nico what feels like a century ago on the patio after he cooked for me.

"Nico," he says.

I spin around to face his twin. And wow. They look exactly alike and yet nothing alike. Nico is who Rafe might have been had their father not thrust the mantle of responsibility on his shoulders at eighteen years old, crushing him beneath an empire he didn't want. They share the same chocolate eyes, the same dark expression. But darkness doesn't cling to Nico like it does to Rafe. He's handsome...but Rafe is beautiful.

I don't think Nico wants to be here. He's tense. Wary. But he's sad too. I want to dislike him for turning his back on Rafe, but I can't. He's hurting too. They were just kids, just teenagers, torn apart by a man who didn't deserve either of them.

"You're his twin?" I ask, my voice soft.

"Yes."

I take three steps toward Nico and then throw my arms around him in a hug, shocking myself. Nico stands frozen for a moment, not moving, and then carefully hugs me back.

"He misses you," I whisper to him. "More than he'll ever admit to you."

"Enough, *tesoro*," Rafe growls, his voice strained.

I huff under my breath, not nearly finished saying what needs to be said to repair their relationship, but at least it's a start. At least he knows Rafe misses him, even if Rafe is too stubborn to admit it. I release Nico and hurry back to Rafe's side.

As soon as I reach him, he wraps an arm around my waist, pulling me into him. He and Nico stare at each other, not speaking. I think Rafe is staking his claim on me again, letting his twin know that I belong to him. Which is ridiculous. I feel nothing for Nico but empathy and compassion. He may be Rafe's twin, but Rafe is the only man in my heart. He'll always be the only man in my heart.

"Tell him the truth," I whisper. "You can't carry it forever. It's time to let it go."

Rafe shakes his head.

"But Rafe," I protest, my heart bleeding for him. Even now, he doesn't believe he deserves forgiveness for what he's done. He truly believes he deserves for Nico to hate him.

"No, Amalia."

"Fine," I mutter, scowling. "Big jerk."

He shakes his head and then presses his lips to my temple. "Go inside before you get yourself in trouble, *mi reinita.*"

I roll my eyes at him. This conversation is far from over. One way or another, I'm going to make him realize that he deserves forgiveness. But for now, I'll let it go. I wrap my arms around him in a tight hug, squeezing as hard as I can. He returns my embrace, holding me close to his chest for a long moment.

I don't want to let him go. I want to stay right here in his arms forever. But I can't.

I release him, leaving him to face his brother.

"You still mad at me?" Rafe asks an hour later, leaning up against the doorjamb in the library, his arms crossed over his chest. He looks tired.

"I was never mad at you," I say, setting my book aside. I haven't read a single page. Honestly, I'm not even sure what book it is. I just picked it up to occupy my hands. Books soothe me. At least they used to soothe me. They haven't done a very good job of that recently.

"You told me to go to hell." His lips twitch.

"Okay, maybe I was a little angry."

His smile grows.

"You threatened to spank me. And tie me to the bed." I narrow my eyes at him. "Rude, by the way."

His gaze rakes over me, slowly heating. "*Tesoro*, you haven't seen rude yet. When I tie to you to the bed —*when*, not if, Amalia—I'll show you exactly how rude I can be. And I guarantee you'll love every fucking minute of it." He pushes away from the door and prowls toward me like a lion, all cool and confident. Sexy as hell. "I won't apologize for worrying about you."

"He's your brother."

"And three days ago, the woman he loves watched me kill the man who assaulted the woman I love," he says, his eyes flashing hellfire. "For all I knew, he was here to kill me."

"I didn't know that," I whisper. "You didn't tell me."

"You didn't need to know." He draws to a stop in front of me, sighing. "You've been through hell already, Amalia. If something happens to you, I won't survive it. Neither will this city. I'll burn it to the fucking ground to avenge you," he growls, his gaze locked on mine. "They'll have to kill me to stop me, *tesoro*."

He means it. I know he does.

"This is all my fault," I say miserably.

"It's not."

He's wrong though. It is my fault.

"I have to tell you something."

"Tell me."

"You aren't going to like it."

"Amalia, tell me."

"Diego knew you would come l-looking for him," I say, my voice shaking. Tears leak from the corners of my eyes, dripping down my cheeks. "We knew you'd bring me here. We p-planned for it."

*I'm sorry. I'm so sorry, Rafe.*

"Why?" he asks, that one word so cold, so hard.

"I was s-supposed to find your books and turn them over to him," I confess.

"Why, Amalia?"

"B-because Diego isn't just a lawyer, Rafe. He's been an FBI informant for years. And Genovese found out. If Diego d-doesn't turn your books over to them and bring you down, Genovese is going to out him," I whisper. "And then he's going to kill me."

"Jesus Christ," Rafe whispers, rocking back on his heels.

"I l-let you bring me h-here to save Diego."

Already, he hates me. Just like I knew he would. Exactly like I deserve. I see it in his eyes. And it hurts so much worse than I thought it would. My heart twists in my chest, tearing itself into miniscule pieces. Acid rushes through my veins, burning me alive. But I haven't even told him all of it yet.

"There's more," I whisper. "Genovese f-forced Diego to kill those men in his territory. He's setting you up. He wants your empire. As soon as you go down, he's going to make his move against your family. He wants everyone to believe you started the war."

"Was any of it real, Amalia?" Rafe asks abruptly, staring at me like he doesn't even know me. Like he's never even seen me until this moment. "Was it all just a fucking act to you?"

"No!" I sob, shaking my head. "No, Rafe. I didn't mean to f-fall in love with you, but I did. I w-wanted to tell you e-everything. I just didn't know how. I didn't want you to h-hate me. I love you. I love you so much. I s-stopped looking for the b-books. I p-p-planned to tell

Diego that I wasn't going to h-help him. Even if it costs me m-my life, I w-won't b-betray you."

He stares at me for a long, silent moment. The look on his face...*God*, it hurts. For days, I've wanted to bring this man to his knees. I've wanted to possess him the way he does me. Instead, I think I just broke him. I see it in his eyes. Defeat. Grief. So much pain.

*What did I do? Oh God. What did I do?*

He strides toward the bookshelves and then stoops down. I watch through tears as he removes a wooden panel I never noticed and then reaches inside. A moment later he pulls out a lockbox and then a stack of journals. He reaches inside again, pulling out another stack.

All this time, they were right here. In the room I've spent most of my time in since I got here. The one place I never thought to look. The one place he hates to come. Of course he hid them here with the ghosts of his past.

He scoops everything up into his arms and then rises to his feet, walking silently toward me. He doesn't say a word as he places them on the sofa beside me.

I cry quietly, chanting *I'm sorry* over and over again.

"Take it, *amore mio*," he says. "Burn it all to the ground." He reaches out, touching my cheek. "You beautiful little liar."

I sob his name, pleading for forgiveness.

But it's already too late. He turns and walks aways.

My heart shatters in my chest.

I cry for hours, sobbing so hard I can't breathe. Daylight slowly slips away, shadows overtaking the room. Night falls. No one comes looking for me. No one intrudes. The house is completely silent. It's as if, for the first time since I arrived here, I'm truly alone.

I pray for Rafe to come back but he doesn't. For hours, I wait. And wait.

Eventually, I realize that he's not coming back. He's gone.

My hand lands on the books he left beside me. These could ruin him. They could destroy everything. Panic seizes me by the throat, stealing my breath. I gather everything up with shaking hands and stumble from the room. The house is dark. Silent.

"Hello?" my voice is raw, little more than a squeak.

No one answers.

I feel my way down the hall, stumbling into the walls as I go.

Somehow, I make it to the kitchen. Light floods the

room when I elbow the switch on. I squeeze my eyes closed against it, my head pounding. My mouth is dry. Everything hurts. I feel worse now than I did when Carmine threw me into the wall. At least that pain was only physical and fleeting. This...well, this goes deeper than that. Half of my heart is missing.

Will it ever be whole again?

No. Not without Rafe it won't.

God, why didn't I tell him sooner? I should have told him when I realized he was already suffering. I knew then that I couldn't go through with it. That he didn't deserve to be dragged down like this. But I said nothing.

He isn't the monster here. I am.

I drop everything onto the island and start prowling through drawers, looking for what I need. I find the lighter hanging on the pantry door. The lighter fluid tucked away in the corner. Flinging the patio doors open, I carry both outside and then go back for the books.

He told me to burn it to the ground.

I will.

Every piece of evidence that can be used against him, I pile into the massive grill stored on the patio and then cover it with lighter fluid. The key to the lockbox is tucked between the pages of one of the registers. I don't look at what they contain. I don't need to know the details.

I know Rafe is a criminal. He's Mafioso, a Made man. I know he launders money and kills people and steals and God only knows what else. This is what is required of him. But I know that's not *who* he is.

We're all more than our mistakes and our worst moments. We're more than our failures and our misdeeds. We're more than our weak moments. We're more than a compilation of the things we've done. We're our hopes and our dreams and our best moments too. We're our strengths and our hearts and our courage. Rafe isn't perfect. But he's suffered enough in his life.

I was born into this world a *principessa*. Rafe made me a queen.

He might not claim me anymore, but I'm *still* his. If no one else is willing to fight for him, I will.

And I won't lose. Not to Genovese. Not to anyone. He may never forgive me. I don't *deserve* his forgiveness. But I will save him. No matter what it takes. I owe him that much.

I dump the lockbox into the grill and then set it aside before pouring lighter fluid over the contents. I soak it all, using every last drop of fluid. And then I set it ablaze.

It goes up with a whoosh, flames shooting into the air. The heat sears me, burning away a little of the chill that settled over me when Rafe walked away. I watch the fire until every last scrap of paper is reduced to ash... and then I go to find Diego.

He and I need to talk. Now.

No one tries to stop me when I walk out the front door. There isn't anyone here *to* stop me. When Rafe left, he took everyone with him. That worries me. I don't know if he sent them to safety or if he sent them to war. I send up a prayer that it's the former, and that I'm able to get to Diego in time to find a way out of this for everyone. He can help me find a solution. He *has* to help me.

Like the house, the guard shack is abandoned.

"This is bad," I whisper, my worry growing.

Did Rafe go after Genovese? After Diego?

I duck inside, praying there's a phone. There isn't one in the house. Rafe won't use a landline. Probably because they're so easy to tap. I nearly sob in relief when I find a phone on the wall in the guard shack.

I dial Diego's number with shaking hands.

His voicemail picks up on the second ring.

"Diego, it's me," I sob. "I t-told Rafe e-everything. I destroyed the e-evidence. I'm s-sorry. Meet me. I'm going to Alvise's. Please meet me there. P-please."

## CHAPTER 11

## *Rafe*

"Rafe, you should go," Mattia says, eyeing me from the doorway.

I ignore his suggestion and reach for the brandy decanter, refilling my glass. I'm not sure why he followed me back here in the first place. He shouldn't have. Everyone else is gone, sent to one of the safe-houses. Hell, I'm not sure why I came back. Part of me —all of me—hoped Amalia would be here waiting for me to return. She wasn't.

My heart fucking *bleeds* at the reminder.

I gave her a choice...and her choice wasn't me. She took everything I handed her, and she left. The fucked up thing about it? I don't even blame her. She did what she had to do to save her brother and herself. If anyone can understand that I can. I made the same decision myself once, didn't I? I risked everything to save Nico.

But goddamn. This one hurts. I can't even seem to drink the pain way.

"Rafe."

"I'm not leaving," I mutter, lifting bleary eyes to Mattia. "Until you find Genovese, or the feds come to arrest me, I'm sitting right here in this fucking chair and drinking. Either get a glass or get out." I turn the light off for good measure, casting the house into complete darkness.

"*Mafankulo*," Mattia snarls, giving up. He stomps out.

"Leave the door open," I call after him, not planning on moving from this chair to open it when the FBI comes knocking.

Mattia grunts what I assume is his opinion of my order. He means well, but he's been pissing me off all day. No wonder Amalia was so crabby this morning. Christ, was it only this morning she was giving me hell about following her around? It feels like another lifetime now.

How did everything go so fucking wrong?

*Genovese.*

I tore his territory apart looking for him today and left a trail of bodies in my wake. I don't know where he's hiding, but I intend to find him. If the FBI doesn't arrest me before I do, I'm taking out his entire motherfucking family before I go down. He never should have come for my family. He damn sure shouldn't have threatened Amalia.

If he wants a war, he just got one. My face will be the last fucking thing he sees before I send him to hell. He can rot next to my father. And then I'm done. With this empire. With this city. With the Mafia. With the whole goddamn thing. It's all pointless anyway.

Without Amalia, it's all fucking pointless.

"Christ," I rasp, draining my glass. My hand shakes as I fumble in the dark for the decanter to pour another. I barely have it to my lips when a soft sound outside reaches me.

"Hello?" a voice calls, followed by a racket in the foyer.

I glance that way to see a single shadow slip into the house. It's too dark to make out much, but I know instantly that this isn't the FBI. They wouldn't send one tiny slip of a girl to take me down. They'd send the fucking cavalry. No. This the same girl who watched me kill Carmine, the student Nico is in love with, the one he came here to discuss today.

I wasn't surprised to see him. I was surprised to realize he's in love with her. She's a student. In a thousand years, I never would have expected the honorable Nico Valentino to fall in love with one of his students. Amalia would be ashamed if she knew what I did today, the way I forced Nico back into the family by holding this girl's safety over his head. As if she were ever in danger.

My own brother believes me capable of killing an innocent girl...and I let him believe it to get him back into my life. I could have told him what really happened back then and absolved myself of his judgement, but to what end? So he could live with twenty years of guilt and regret? Sometimes, the truth is too goddamn painful to tell, the consequences too goddamn real to risk.

I've never understood that as acutely as I do right now.

"Stupid invisible doorstep," Norah mutters, stumbling into the foyer. "Stupid dark house. Why aren't there any stupid lights on?"

"Because I was enjoying my solitude," I say drily.

"Christ on a cracker!" she shouts.

I sigh, not even remotely prepared for whatever conversation she's here to have with me now.

"Mr. Valentino?

"You're not the FBI."

"Um, no." She takes a shuffling step toward me and then stops.

"Pity.

"My name is..."

"Norah Bishop," I say when she hesitates.

She doesn't say anything.

I give up and reach for the lamp, switching it on. She stands frozen just outside of the living room, her feet rooted to the floor. Her eyes are wide, her face pale. She's terrified out of her mind, but she came here anyway. Interesting. She's a curvy little doll with bright eyes and pale blonde hair. She's a year or two younger than Amalia.

They're both too fucking young to be caught up in any of this...and yet they are.

"Are you okay?" she asks.

I stare at her, not speaking. Three nights ago, she watched me murder a man. Now, she's asking if I'm okay? She's just like Nico.

"I mean, obviously you're not okay. You're sitting in

the dark drinking whiskey," she mutters, desperate to fill the silence. I don't think silence is in her nature. "No one sits in the dark and drinks whiskey if they're having a good day."

"Why are you here, Norah?" I ask quietly, not correcting her about my alcohol of choice.

She snaps her mouth closed, watching me intently.

"You have a tendency to show up in places you shouldn't," I say. "Does my brother know you're here?"

"No," she whispers and then lick her lips. "I mean yes."

"You're a terrible liar, Miss Bishop," I mutter, raising my glass to my lips to hide a smile, my first all day. I...like this girl. She's brave as hell. She'll be good for Nico. "He would have tied you to his bed before he let you come here on your own."

"I snuck out," she admits, wiping her hands on her pants.

"Why?"

"Because I wanted to talk to you."

I lower my glass again without taking a sip. "You wanted to talk to me."

"Yes."

"Go on then. Talk."

Amalia would love her. They'd be two peas in a pod.

"I..." She huffs out a breath, clearly searching for words. "I came to make you a deal."

"You want to make a deal with me."

Oh, yes. Amalia would definitely love this girl. She has fire in her, and spirit.

"Yes," she says, squaring her shoulders. "You took your father's side to save Nico."

I blink, caught off guard.

"You knew he wasn't cut out for this life," she says, stumbling over the words in her haste to get them out. "So you offered yourself up to your father in exchange for his freedom."

"Interesting theory."

"Am I wrong?"

"Does it matter?"

"It matters to me," I say. "It matters to you. I think it'd matter to Nico too."

I take a sip of my brandy, not responding. She didn't tell him. Why?

"He misses you. He misses your other brothers too. But he feels like you guys abandoned him."

"Is that why you're here? To try to fix this family?" I arch one brow in question.

"No. I'm here for Nico." She pauses, fidgeting nervously. "If you call off your deal with him, I won't tell anyone what I saw. I'll carry your secret to my grave. No one will ever know what happened that night."

"Why?" I ask.

"Because I love him just as much as you do," she whispers, her voice shaking with emotion. "Because I'd do anything to save him from this world, just like you did. He doesn't belong in this world, Rafe. You know he doesn't."

I take another drink, pain ripping through me. She gambled with her life by coming here, not knowing if I'd kill her or not. But she did it for Nico anyway. She and Amalia are exactly alike. For the people they love, they're willing to risk everything. Unfortunately for me, I just wasn't one of those people for Amalia. She chose her brother. She chose self-preservation. She didn't trust that I could keep her safe. And that's what fucking kills me. She didn't trust me to protect her.

I would have torn this fucking world apart for her... and it wasn't enough.

"Go home, Norah," I say, glancing away.

"No."

"No?"

"Not until I know Nico is safe," she says, digging her heels in. "Leave him alone, Rafe. I'll keep your secret."

Jesus Christ.

"You two are a pair," I mutter, rubbing my forehead. I'm fucking exhausted. "Twelve hours ago, he was here telling me to leave you alone. Only his version of this speech included considerably more threats."

"He's passionate."

I snort. That's one way of putting it.

"If it were you, wouldn't you do whatever you had to do to save the person you love?" she presses, refusing to give up.

"I'd tear the fucking world apart for her," I rasp, meaning every word.

Norah gasps quietly.

"But as I recently discovered, she doesn't feel the same." I tip my glass to my lips, draining it.

"I bet that's not true," she whispers, her face falling.

"You'd lose that bet then."

"Do you...want to talk about it?" she asks.

I laugh abruptly. This girl is unbelievable. "You came here to save my brother from my clutches, and now you're asking if I want to talk about my love life?"

"It's not you I'm trying to save him from. It's your world. Your job. The things you do." She waves her hand in the air as if to indicate what she means. "I'm sorry. I don't know the appropriate term here. I just know that Nico is a good man with a big heart and a bright future. If you take that away from him, he'll lose himself."

"You're so sure I want to take something from him. Why?"

"I..." She trails off, her brows furrowing. "I guess I don't know that," she admits. "I guess I just assumed you wanted to pull him back into the...things...you do."

"Did."

"Huh?"

"The things I did," I mutter, shaking my head. "It's a long, sad story that I don't feel much like telling at the moment. I'm not accepting your deal, Miss Bishop. Go home to my brother where you belong."

"No."

I flick my gaze in her direction, my patience running out. "That's the second time you've told me no," I say, my voice soft. "I wouldn't test my patience by saying it a third time."

"I'm not afraid of you."

"You should be," I growl. "I've killed people for less."

"I remember. I was there," she snaps, scowling.

"And yet I'm still standing here. You may think you're this big scary monster, but you're a man just like anyone else. You're a little crankier than most of them, but you're still just a man. And I think I could say just about anything to you and still walk out of here alive because you still love your brother and you and I both know that killing me will destroy any chance you have of ever getting him back into your life."

I stare at her through slit lids for a long moment. For twenty years, people in this city have tiptoed around me, treating me like the big, bad wolf. And then I met Amalia. She was never afraid of me, not even once. Now this little slip of a girl is reading me the riot act too. Either I've lost my touch, or women truly are the most terrifying things on this earth.

I'm pretty sure it's the latter.

"I can see why he fell for you," I say, my expression softening. "You're both stubborn."

"We're scientists."

"Clearly." I reach for the decanter beside the lamp to refill my glass. "But I'm not letting you walk out of here because I'm worried about destroying our relationship. It's occurred to me that I fucked that up a long time ago. There is no taking it back now."

"I don't know what that means," she admits.

"It means..." I sigh, replacing the stopper on the decanter. "It means you're free, Miss Bishop. It means he's free too. Tell the world what you saw or don't. I don't fucking care anymore."

"Oh." She frowns. "Why not?"

"The girl I love is with the FBI right now, turning

over everything she has on me," I say. "This time tomorrow, I'll be in cuffs." Or dead. Either way, it's over for me.

"Oh. Wow. Um, that's a lot."

"Indeed." I raise my glass to my lips again and sip. "As interesting as this visit has been, I'd prefer to wallow in misery alone. So, please, Miss Bishop, go home."

"What's her name?" she asks, her voice soft.

"Amalia."

"Amalia," she repeats. "It's a beautiful name."

"She's a beautiful girl."

"You really love her?"

I nod, staring at...nothing. Feeling nothing.

"I'm sorry," Norah whispers. "I won't pretend to know what happened between you or how she feels about you. But I think if you love her, she must be someone worth loving. I don't think you would have fallen for her if she wasn't. Maybe she'll surprise you."

"Maybe," I mutter, leaving it at that. Is she worth loving? God, yeah. Would I do it again even knowing how it ends? In a heartbeat. A moment with her is worth an eternity in hell. A single moment.

"Good luck, Rafe," Norah whispers, turning to leave.

"Miss Bishop."

She pauses at the door.

"You're good for him."

"He's good for me too."

"I'll call you a cab."

"Thank you." She slips out the door, leaving me in peace.

My peace is short lived.

Not even twenty minutes after Norah leaves, Nico shows up.

"Norah!" he shouts, flinging open the front door so hard it crashes against the wall.

"She isn't here."

He spins toward me, eyes wild, breathing hard. Panic clings to him, fear heavy in the air around him. He's terrified. I know the look. I'm pretty sure I wore it when I heard Amalia scream the day Carmine tried to kidnap her.

"Where is she?" Nico growls.

"I sent her back to you twenty minutes ago," I say, still sipping from my glass. Just when I think the liquor has dulled the worst of the pain, I find a new depth to explore. I passed drunk a glass or three ago, but my mind still feels all too clear. "That is what you wanted, is it not?"

Why did she leave? Fuck. Why did I let her go?

"You sent her back to me," he repeats. "Unharmed?"

A rough bark of laughter rips from my lips. I glance at him, my emotions raw. My mind spinning in circles. Amalia's beautiful face hangs like a ghost behind my eyes, haunting me. "My own twin questions the worth of my soul," I mutter. "No wonder she left."

"Who? Norah?"

"Amalia." I take another drink and then sigh. "If I'm lucky, the feds will be here soon to dismantle this fucking empire. It's a noose around my neck. And I was stupid enough to believe it wouldn't claim my life."

Nico eyes me warily. "What happened?"

"I just told you," I growl, not nearly drunk enough yet to rehash this again. But I do anyway. "She left me. She was a beautiful little liar. She made me fall for her, made me need her, and then she just fucking...left me."

"Jesus," he whispers.

"She was a plant, a mole. I'm not even sure her name is Amalia." I laugh again, the sound bitter, mocking. "I fell for it, brother. Like a fucking sinking stone. Ah, well. My downfall should make you happy. It's what you've always wanted."

"I never wanted that," he mutters.

"No?" I eye him over the rim of my glass, surprised. "I wouldn't blame you if you did. You're in love with her. Norah."

"Yes."

"She's a persistent little thing, isn't she?"

"She's everything," he says simply.

"She's free. Both of you. Our deal is off."

Nico cocks his head to the side, eyeing me. "Why?"

Why?

"Because I'm not the heartless bastard you think I am. I'm not as far gone as you think I am. She was never in danger from me, brother. I don't kill innocent women, regardless of what you think of me."

"She watched you kill someone."

"The man who attacked the woman *I* love," I rasp. "That's who she watched me kill. Had she gone to the police, I wouldn't have raised a hand to stop her. I would have accepted my fate with a smile on my face. The motherfucker deserved to die for the things he's done. No jury would have ever convicted."

"Jesus," Nico whispers, clearly shocked. He never stopped to ask who I killed or why. He never wondered if there was a reason. His moral compass points firmly north and never deviates. Murder is murder, plain and simple.

My moral compass is an inverted pendulum, swinging back and forth. I exist in the gray area where there are no moral absolutes. There's simply *Omertà*. The code of silence. We handle our own problems, mete out our own justice, and deal with shit our own way. I've never killed someone who didn't deserve it by our laws. I've never targeted a woman or child. I've never been a fucking rat. Everything else is negotiable.

"I wanted you back in my life, even if I had to manipulate you into it," I say, my voice soft. "Maybe that makes me the bastard you've always thought I was.

I don't know. But that's over with. You're free. Go live your life. Take care of your girl. Be happy. You deserve it more than the rest of us."

Nico stares at me for a moment like I have two heads. "If you love her, fight for her."

"You're not hearing me, brother. She's gone. Out. Done. And so I am," I say, spelling it out for him. "She has everything they need to nail me to the wall. I gave it all to her."

"You *gave* it to her?"

I nod. "Some shit is more important than all of this. Some people matter more than all of this. I just wish like hell I'd realized that twenty years ago. Before I lost my brother." I exhale a breath, and then say what I should have twenty fucking years ago. "For what it's worth, I'm sorry."

For a long time, Nico doesn't say anything. He stands rooted in place, just looking at me. I don't know what he's thinking. When we were kids, I could read him like a book. It's not so easy now. We've had twenty years of silence between us. Twenty years of anger. He thought I abandoned him. I thought I was saving him. Maybe I should have told him the truth a long time ago, let him make his own choice instead of making it for him. I don't know.

What I do know is that Amalia was right...I can't carry it forever. Twenty years is long enough.

"You didn't lose me," Nico rasps.

I meet his gaze, gratitude and grief rushing through me in tandem. My head bows beneath the weight of it. For the first time since our mother died...I cry.

## CHAPTER 12

*Amalia*

**A**lvise's house sits on the outer edge of what used to be my family's territory. Lorenzo Valentino swallowed up the area after he killed my father, claiming it as his own. Everyone loyal to my father fled, leaving Lorenzo to move his men into the area. This neighborhood is small, quiet. Not much goes on here anymore.

Most of the Mafioso who lived here died a long time ago or moved on. Alvise's house has been empty for years. I guess it belongs to me and Diego now, but it'll always be Alvise's in my mind. I lived here for two days before he moved me to the far side of Chicago. No one even knew I was here. They slipped me in under cover of darkness...and slipped me back out the same way.

It's probably the worst possible place for Diego to meet me, but it's the only place I could get to on foot from Rafe's without asking for help. I figured flagging down a car and asking for a ride would be like leaving a flaming arrow in the sky pointing the way to my brother.

I can talk to Diego here, try to make him see reason. I have no idea what I'm going to say. I have no idea if he'll listen. All I know is that I have to try. I don't want to lose him, but I can't lose Rafe. I'll fight whatever battles I have to fight to earn his forgiveness, for however long I have to fight them.

I slip through the back door of Alvise's house into the kitchen, pocketing the key Diego hid under one of the flagstones.

"Diego?" I call into the dark. "Are you here?"

He doesn't answer.

I sigh heavily. Of course he's not here yet. It hasn't even been half an hour since I called him. There's no telling where he is or how long it'll take him to get here. It could be hours.

Feeling my way to the sink, I turn it on and wash my face and then cup my hands under the water to take a drink. Thanks to all the crying, I feel like I have razorblades lodged in my throat, gnawing at it. The cool water soothes the worst of it. It doesn't make *me* feel better though.

Nothing short of feeling Rafe's arms around me again will do that. Until I see him again, *talk* to him again, I'm not going to be okay. There's still so much I need to say to him. I didn't get a chance to tell him the worst of it before he left. He still doesn't know about my father. Once he does, he may never forgive me. But even if he never wants to see me again, even if he hates me for the rest of my life, I'll never regret burning those documents. I'll never regret refusing to sacrifice him to save Diego and myself.

I love him with everything in me. With everything I am. There won't ever be anyone else for me. How could there be? My *soul* belongs to him. I gave it to him willingly, without reservation. I'll never want it back. If all I'll have of him for the rest of my life are memories, I'll find a way to survive on them. I'll never replace his touch with another. Not ever.

I feel my way through the kitchen and into the living room. The moonlight filtering through the large bay windows guides the way. I don't turn on any lights, not wanting to draw any attention to the house. I don't know if Rafe still wants to kill Diego or not, but until I know for sure, I need to be careful. Forcing a confrontation between them right now seems likely to end in disaster for all of us. Especially once I tell Diego that I'm in love with Rafe.

He's going to be furious. He'll rant and rave and swear that Rafe messed with my head. As if I'm not perfectly capable of making up my own mind. As if he didn't teach me everything he knows about protecting myself. But Diego is overprotective and stubborn and never sees reason. And he loves me. I'm his baby sister, his only family.

And Rafe...well, Rafe is the man he's hated since he was fifteen years old. Dario Marchesi may have been a horrible man to the rest of the world, but to Diego he was a father. Maybe not a great one, but a father, nonetheless. And Rafe is the man who killed him. Diego's had fifteen years to hate him. It's going to take more than fifteen minutes to undo it.

I pull the dust cover off the old sofa and curl up in a ball to wait for Diego. My eyes drift closed, exhaustion quickly pulling me under.

A soft sound jerks me awake. I sit bolt upright on the sofa, blinking.

Rain slides down the windows, silvery storm clouds obscuring the moon. I have no idea how long I've been asleep, or what time it is, but it's still dark out.

The sound comes again, like a shuffling from the kitchen.

Diego's here. *Finally!*

I jump up from the sofa and hurry that way, tears of relief welling in my eyes. God, it feels like it's been four years since I saw him last. I miss him so much. Not being able to talk to him, not knowing if he was okay...I couldn't allow myself to think about it or I would have cracked. But knowing that he's here now feels like a weight falling from my shoulders.

"Diego," I cry, racing into the kitchen.

I realize my mistake a moment too late.

The elderly man in the kitchen isn't Diego. Neither is the giant at his side.

"Genovese," I whisper, staring in horror.

*Oh, no. Oh, no.*

Genovese meets my gaze, smiling. "Ah, *principessa*. There you are."

Battista lunges for me.

## CHAPTER 13

*Rafe*

W hen the pounding on the front door starts, I'm no longer drunk. I'm not entirely sober either. Regret pulses in my chest as I haul myself to my feet and stumble through the foyer to let them in before they break down the door. I knew they were coming, but I really fucking hoped it'd be after Mattia found Genovese so I could kill him slow.

I pull the door open, and then blink.

*"Che cazzo?"* *What the fuck?*

"Where is she?" Diego growls, aiming a pistol at me. The right side of his face is a mess of healing bruises. Courtesy of Genovese, I'm guessing.

"Get the fucking gun out of my face," I say calmly.

"Where is she?" he roars in response.

What little patience I have left after the day I've had flees. My blood pressure spikes, my temper erupting. I grab him by the throat and drag him into the house, knocking the gun from his hand in the process. He takes a swing at me, the edge of his fist glancing off the side of my face.

I slam him up against the wall.

He tries to hit me again.

"Calm the fuck down before I put you down," I snarl, cutting off his air supply. "You came to my house, waving a fucking gun in my face. The only goddamn reason you're still breathing is *because of her*. What do you mean where is she? She's supposed to be with you." I relax my grip slightly, allowing him to speak.

"She left a voicemail. Crying." He glowers at me. "She wanted to meet at Alvise's place. When I got there, she wasn't there."

"If I let you go, are you going to piss me off?" I ask.

He stares at me, hatred burning in his eyes.

"*Mafankulo*," I curse. "You want to kill me? Fine. I'm not too fucking keen on keeping you alive at the moment either. You've been pissing me off for two weeks. But right now, none of that shit matters because your sister isn't with me, and she isn't with you either. And Genovese tried to kidnap her from here three days ago. So you can either stow your shit and help me find her or get the fuck out of my way because until she's safe, nothing else fucking matters to me. *Nothing*!"

"Goddammit," he swears. "He tried to kidnap her?"

"Three days ago," I mutter.

He grits his teeth, eyeing me like he isn't sure if he believes me or not. And then he reluctantly holds his hands up in a gesture of surrender.

I slowly release my hold on him, stepping back.

"He's offering millions to anyone who brings her to

him," I say after a moment, watching him intently. "Any idea why?"

He hesitates.

"I already know about your deal with him to bring me down." I scowl, still furious about that. Diego is a rat, an informant. He's been working with Genovese against my family. If I didn't need him, I'd put a bullet between his eyes right now. If he weren't Amalia's brother, I wouldn't even regret it. But I do need him, and he is her brother. That's the only thing keeping him alive. "Amalia told me everything, so don't try to bullshit me, Butera. Why does he think she's someone else?"

"I want your word that you're helping me kill Genovese regardless of who she is," he says.

"Oh, I'm definitely killing Genovese. I'm taking out his entire goddamn family if that's what it takes," I vow. "As soon as I find that *brutto figlio di puttana bastardo*, he's dead. I'll swear whatever oath you want me to swear."

"He thinks she's Serafina Cerrito."

"Why does he think that?" I ask, watching his expression carefully.

He holds my gaze, not flinching. "Because she is."

"Jesus Christ," I whisper, stunned. The scars on my abdomen burn. I place my hand over them on instinct, drawing Diego's attention. I quickly drop my hand back to my side, curling it into a fist. She's... Jesus Christ.

Her father murdered my mother in cold blood. He nearly killed me. My father went on the warpath in retaliation. He systematically wiped out her entire family one by one. He saved her parents for last. It took him seven years to get to them. Their baby daughter is the only one who survived the fire that consumed their home.

Once he found out she survived, he was furious. I think he would have hunted her down and finished the job had I let him. The one and only time I defied my father was the day he found out she survived. I refused to go after her. He raged for a while and then stormed out. When he returned a few hours later, we never spoke of her again. I always assumed, he'd finally cooled down and saw reason. She was a baby, a two-year-old child. It wasn't her war.

"Does she know?" I ask Diego.

"Does it matter?" he challenges.

Does it? Does knowing who she is change a goddamn thing?

It changes everything. She's a *principessa*, the only remaining member of the Cerrito family in Chicago. Even with no territory, no home, and no family, she's worth millions. The other families will tear the city apart to get their hands on her, her name, and her fortune. That's why Genovese wanted her so badly, and why he was so fucking worried about her being in my care.

But does any of this change the way I feel about *her*? That's not even a question. My heart beats for her and always will. Do I like the thought of her keeping this from me? Fuck no. But I can't judge her for it when I've done the same thing for twenty years. I kept the truth from Nico, trying to shield him from it. She did what she thought she had to do to protect herself. And, just maybe, to protect me too.

"No," I say softly, holding his gaze. "It doesn't matter."

Our lives are intwined in ways that defy description. They cross and intersect at so many different points, all leading to this same place, to this same inevitable conclusion. If that isn't a sign, I don't know what is. We were always supposed to end up here. We were always meant for one another. Maybe it ends happy for us. Maybe it ends in bloodshed. I don't know. But I do know this...however it ends for us, it ends together.

I'm getting my girl back. And I'm killing Tommaso Genovese. Right now.

Diego, Mattia, and I find Genovese hiding in the last place anyone would expect to find him: The deli halfway between my territory and his. It's the perfect hiding place, the one place in this city no one would expect him to go. It's smart, I'll give him that. But I didn't make it to the top by being easily outwitted. The deli is one of the first places I decide to check.

*I'm coming, amore mio. I'm coming.*

The one problem is the ten men guarding the block. And those are the ones we know about. Who knows how many others Genovese has tucked into hiding places we haven't yet found? Battista is guarding the front door...the last line of defense. Genovese isn't taking any chances.

"Find every single one of his men and kill them," I tell Mattia, my voice ice cold. I'm not taking prisoners tonight. I'm not showing mercy. This will be the first and last time anyone comes for Amalia. Anyone else who thinks to try me will think again after tonight. "Load every single one of them up and leave them on his son's doorstep."

Mattia grins, a vicious, savage grin. "I'll call Coda and rally the troops." His gaze flicks to Diego in the rearview mirror. "What about him?"

"He's coming with me," I mutter.

Diego grunts.

"You sure about that?" Mattia asks. "I can leave his body behind too."

"He's coming with me," I repeat.

Mattia shrugs and slips out of the SUV.

"You're in love with her," Diego says a moment later.

"You're just figuring that out?" I glance at Diego through the mirror to find him watching me.

"I don't approve."

"I don't remember asking for your approval."

His jaw clenches, groaning under the strain.

"I killed your father," I say quietly, not lying to him. "He broke the rules and paid the price I set. I won't pretend it was right or just or fair. I did what I did because it was my call to make. I won't try to justify or rationalize it to you. You can hate me for it, that's your right. I won't take that from you. But I love your sister. I believe she feels the same about me." *Please, don't let me be wrong,* I pray. I don't think I am though. I listened to the voicemail she left Diego. She told him she was calling it off, that she destroyed the evidence. She chose me. "I'll protect her above all things, love her above all things. Don't make her choose between us."

"It seems to me like she already fucking chose," he growls.

Jesus Christ. Is he ever anything less than hostile?

"She's your sister," I say, my patience dwindling. "Have a little fucking respect. She's earned that much from you. Don't think I've forgotten that you're the reason she's in this mess to begin with. Don't think I've forgotten that you're the reason Genovese got his hands on her. Don't think I've forgotten that *you let her walk into the home of your enemy to save your own life.*" I take a breath, trying to get my temper under control before I decide to kill him for that and ask her forgiveness later. He never should have let her walk into my house under my guard. *Especially* not knowing what I'd do once I knew who she really is. I want to kill him for that alone. "I don't give a flying fuck if you like me or not. If you break her heart, you'll answer to me."

"The same goes for you," he snarls. "Break her heart, and I'll spend the rest of my life making yours a living hell."

"Agreed."

He sits back in his seat. And then he laughs abruptly. "You're dumber than you look if you think anyone *lets* Amalia do anything," he says. "No one tells her what to do."

I chuckle because he's not lying about that. She takes orders from no one.

*Mafankulo.*

Diego and I stop laughing at the same time, looking at each other in the mirror. His grim, worried expression is an exact replica of mine.

'We've got to get her out of there," I mutter.

He nods silently.

CHAPTER 14

## *Amalia*

"Y ou should eat something, *principessa*," Genovese says, pushing a plate of fruit toward me across the scarred wooden tabletop with one hand. Despite the age spots dotting his skin, he's spry, seemingly healthy. He keeps smiling at me.

"I'm not hungry," I say, turning my face away to stare at the wall. We're in some sort of deli a short drive from Rafe's. He brought me here a few hours ago. I think he has people watching the place, but I'm not sure. He and Battista haven't said much around me. What little I've been able to overhear hasn't been much use.

All I know is that Rafe is looking for Genovese, and they don't think he'll look here. Which means I'm on my own. I have to rescue myself. Somehow. There isn't much here that'll be of use. The deli is old. I don't believe it's a functioning business any longer.

Is this the place Rafe told me about? The deli where they meet for sit-downs?

Genovese makes a sound of protest in the back of his throat that sets my teeth on edge. He's been playing good cop all night, being overly solicitous. It has me ready to crawl out of my skin. This is the same man who sent Diego home covered in blood and bruises two weeks ago. The same man who sent Carmine to kidnap me. The same one who has carefully orchestrated every move of this entire nightmare, shifting us around on the board like his own personal pawns.

If there are any monsters in Chicago, it's not Rafe. It's him.

And yet he acts like a kind, caring old man.

I'm not falling for it.

"Come now, Serafina," he says. "Eat something."

"That's not my name," I growl, whipping around to glare at him. "My name is Amalia Santiago."

"Amalia," he repeats, his lips curving into the hint of a smile. "Your mother's name."

I just stare at him, not speaking. Not confirming anything. Whatever he wants from me, he's not getting it. He'll have to pry the truth from my corpse. I don't trust him or his nice guy act.

"You don't trust me," he says as if reading my mind.

*Trust* him? I'm pretty sure I hate him.

"You threatened to kill me. You offered a bounty for me. You tried to have me kidnapped," I remind him. "You tried to use my brother to destroy Rafe." I end my list there, though there are a thousand other things I could add to it, like the fact that he wants to destroy Rafe at all, and the fact that Rafe hates me because of him. Or the fact that I stabbed a man because of him.

Or that Rafe had to kill that same man. Like I said, it's a long list.

"I see." He pushes the plate closer to me. "You were never in any danger from me, Serafina." He holds up a hand to silence me when I open my mouth. "My apologies, *principessa*. Amalia. I'm not trying to hurt you. I'm merely trying to offer you a...deal."

I blink at him, caught off guard. "You want to offer me a deal?"

"I want you to marry my grandson," he says bluntly.

"I..." I open my mouth and then close it. Open and then close it. Out of everything I thought might come out of his mouth, that one didn't make the list. "You want me to marry your grandson?"

"You're the sole remaining heir to your family's dynasty, my dear. The Cerrito name, the Cerrito legacy, the coffers, it's all yours," he says, eyeing me shrewdly. "It won't do you any good on your own. But a Cerrito-Genovese alliance?" His eyes light up. "Now that would be real power. Perhaps enough to install a new *Capo dei capi* once Valentino is out of the picture."

"I..." I gape at him. "You want me to marry your grandson."

"I want the power, girl," he snaps. "Valentino's had it long enough. He's done nothing with it but subjugate and crush us. We used to be gods among men. Now, we answer to him. Nothing happens without his consent or approval. There are no power struggles, no wars between families, no alliances. We're expected to behave like good little soldiers and stay in our places."

His eyes gleam with hatred. "I'm not a soldier. I don't bow."

He's mad because he can't make war?

Diego was right. This man is crazy.

"Thank you for the offer, but I'm going to have to decline," I say as politely as possible, wary of setting him off. "I can't marry your grandson."

"It wasn't an offer."

"You said you wanted to make me a deal."

"I lied," he snaps, no longer the solicitous old man, but the ruthless, heartless criminal. "You're marrying my grandson. Your father promised. I intend to hold him to it."

"My father...?" I gape at him in shock. "My father is dead."

"He sold you to me before you were even born," Genovese says with a wave of his hand. "The deal was struck the day he found out you were a girl. Lorenzo may have taken him out, but you're still alive. Imagine my surprise when you practically fell into my lap. The deal still stands. You're marrying my grandson."

I bite back the hot retort on the tip of my tongue, swallowing it even though it threatens to choke me. Yelling at this man isn't going to do me any favors. I need to move carefully, think this through rationally, calmly. It's the only way I'm going to find a way out of this.

Is there a way out? Even if I somehow manage to get past this man, Battista is outside. I might be a match for an elderly man. I'm no match for a freaking giant. And who knows how many men are waiting past him. I should have stayed at Rafe's. For once in my life, I should have listened.

*Rafe!* Of course. Why didn't I think of that sooner?

I don't need to get out. I just need to get Rafe *in*. If I can get him close enough to Genovese, he'll kill him. He won't lose. Rafe never loses, especially not when it comes to his family.

"I'll marry your grandson, but I want something first," I blurt, my heart racing.

Genovese eyes me oddly.

"I want to see Rafe." I curl my hands into fists, scoring my palms with my nails to steady myself. I can't mess this up. If Genovese doesn't believe me, it's over for me. It's over for all of us. And all the king's horses and all the king's men won't be able to put us back together again. "I've spent eight days listening to him tell everyone that I belong to him as if he could just make it so. I want to see the look on his face when he realizes that I belonged to someone else all along."

Before Genovese even smiles, I know I have him. I know we've won.

Genovese doesn't waste any time making the call. He can taste victory. He thinks he's won. I force myself to nibble on the fruit while we wait for Rafe. My stomach threatens to rebel, but I refuse to give in to the bile crawling up my throat. I refuse to lose to this horrible man. So I nibble, and I smile, and I pretend that this man is my savior.

Time passes so slowly I want to scream. Fifteen minutes crawl by. It takes Rafe twenty minutes to get to me. When he steps through the door, he's alone.

He looks like he's been to hell and back, but he's still my dark prince. So damn beautiful.

I nearly sob in relief at the sight of him.

His dark gaze sweeps across the room. It lands on me, cold and hard and distant. But I see a flicker and I know *my* Rafe is in there. The devil and the lover, the impossibly complicated man who owns me, body and soul. I haven't lost him. Not yet.

And then I see the gun in his hands.

My body sags in relief, a whimper escaping me.

*It's over. It's finally over.*

"What is this?" Genovese demands, spotting it at the same time. "Where's Battista?"

"Bleeding out in the gutter," Rafe says, his voice cold. His expression darkens with murderous intent as he turns it on Genovese. "You can thank her brother for that."

Diego is here too? Oh, thank you God.

A choked sob escapes me.

Genovese plants his hands on the tabletop as if to give himself leverage to hoist himself to his feet.

"Sit the fuck down, old man," Rafe says, his voice soft. He points the gun at him, his aim steady. His eyes drift to me. "Come here, *tesoro*."

I fly across the deli to his side, my feet barely touching the floor.

"Are you all right, *amore mio*?" he asks.

I sob in response, unable to form words.

"Did he hurt you, Amalia?"

I shake my head.

"Thank God," Rafe whispers, his eyes drifting closed. They spring open again immediately. He reaches out to touch my cheek. "Wait outside for me, *amore, mio*."

"Rafe."

"Wait outside, Amalia."

I turn toward the door to obey his quiet order and then pause, turning back to face Genovese. He's still sitting in the same spot, watching us with hatred stamped across his face. He knows he's lost though. I see it in his gaze.

"My name is Amalia Santiago and I belong to Rafael Valentino," I tell him, my voice shaking. "No one else has a claim on me. Not you. Not your grandson. Not my father. No one. You don't deserve power, Mr. Genovese. And you don't deserve whatever mercy Rafe shows you tonight. You're a monster."

"Amalia, go," Rafe says. I hear the hint of amusement in his voice though. And the pride.

I slip out the door. It's still raining, but dawn lights

the horizon, burning away the endless, nightmarish night. I catch sight of my brother, standing guard beside the door.

"Diego!" I burst into a fresh round of tears at the sight of him, flinging myself into his arms.

He catches me, pulling me roughly into his arms. I crack, overwhelmed by...everything. This day has been a waking nightmare from start to finish, and I don't even know how or where to begin processing it. All I know is that Diego and Rafe are safe, alive, and somehow, they're both here now. Together.

"Baby sister," Diego rasps, rocking me back and forth while I sob into his shoulder.

"I'm s-s-sorry," I cry. "I'm sorry."

"You have nothing to be sorry for," he growls, squeezing me tight.

"I b-burned all the e-evidence," I remind him, wiping my face on his shirt. And then I say the hard part, the part I'm pretty sure will cost me one of the two men I love. But I just spent a day in hell without Rafe. I won't survive a lifetime of the same. It'll break my heart to lose Diego, but I won't survive losing Rafe. "I'm...I l-love him, Diego."

Diego tenses and then breathes out a ragged curse. "Fuck. I know."

"You know?" I pull back to look at him, sniffling.

"You burned the evidence that would have saved your life, Lia," he says, frustration burning in his eyes. "I figured you only do some shit like that for someone you love."

"Genovese never planned to kill me," I mutter. "I

think he just told you that to motivate you. He needed me alive to marry his grandson."

"What the fuck?" Diego asks, his brows furrowing in confusion.

"It's a long story."

"I got time."

The single gunshot makes me jump.

"Maybe I don't have time," Diego mutters warily.

We stand in silence for several long moments. My heart is in my throat. I don't think I draw a full breath until Rafe steps out of the deli, pulling the door closed behind him.

His eyes lock on mine. They aren't cold this time. They're burning hot, blazing with emotion. It's deliverance and devotion, powerful and bright.

Just like that, I'm crying again. Sobbing so hard I can't breathe anyway.

"Amalia, *tesoro*," he whispers, holding his arms open for me.

I hit him like a meteor, flinging him back a step.

His arms close around me, a shudder wracking his powerful frame.

"Don't let me go," I plead through sobs, wrapping myself around him, trying to fuse us into one being. "Please don't ever let me go."

"Never," he swears, his lips seeking mine. "Never, *amore mio*."

"We should talk," I whisper to Rafe as he strips us both naked with a single-minded focus. We're home, the events of the night behind us. Mattia is dealing with the aftermath. Diego stayed behind to help. For the first time in what feels like years, Rafe and I are completely alone.

I've never been so nervous. Not even the very first night he brought me here.

"Later," Rafe grunts, stripping my shirt off over my head.

"Rafe."

"Amalia."

"Dammit, Rafe."

"*Amore mio*," he says, brushing his lips across my forehead. "There is nothing you need to say that can't wait until you've had some sleep. You're barely standing upright."

He's right, but...

"Alessandro Cerrito was my father," I blurt. I've

been trying to tell him for days. I'm not putting it off for a single second longer. He deserves to know now. Before anything else happens and it gets put on the back burner again. I don't think I can crawl into this bed naked with him only for him to turn away from me later.

He lifts his gaze to mine, unflinching. "And Lorenzo Valentino was mine."

Hope sprouts in my chest, seedlings threatening to bloom.

"My father killed your mother," I say, too afraid to let them grow. "He shot you."

"And mine murdered your entire family." Something shifts through his eyes. Regret? Guilt? Remorse? "He wanted to kill you. Did you know that? He was not happy you survived the fire. He demanded that I finish the job." He brushes his hands along my sides, pulling me closer as if to protect me from the memory. "I refused. It was the first time I defied an order."

"I..." I swallow. "Really?"

He nods. "You aren't responsible for your father's crimes, *tesoro*. You weren't even born when he committed them. You didn't deserve to be punished for them." He sighs softly, shame burning in his gaze. "If anyone carries blame here, it's me. I didn't stop him from killing your parents. I wanted your father to suffer for what he did."

I reach out, running my hand across the scars on his abdomen. "He deserved to suffer," I whisper. Maybe I'm a terrible daughter, I don't know. I wish I'd gotten a chance to know my mother. But I feel no affinity for the man who shot Rafe. I feel no affinity for the man who sold me to Genovese. My loyalty lies with the innocent little boy who suffered unimaginably at his hands...and for the broken, complicated man that little boy grew into. My heart is with him. Always.

"An eye for an eye makes the whole world blind," Rafe murmurs, running his hands up and down my sides again. He stops at the band of my panties, toying with it.

"Then find a different way. You're the king. Make your own rules."

He eyes me for a minute and then smiles a purely wicked, devilish smile. "I just made one."

"Yeah? Let's hear it then."

"My queen isn't allowed to wear clothes in this room," he says.

"Do you still..." I swallow hard, my heart beating a thousand miles a minute. "Do you still want me to be your queen?"

"I never stopped," he rasps.

"I hurt you," I whisper, tears filling my eyes at the reminder. They drip down my cheeks unchecked. "I'm so sorry, Rafe. I never meant to hurt you. I swear to you, I decided not to follow through with it almost immediately. The night you had the nightmare, I knew I couldn't do it. I stopped looking for your books and started looking for a way to save you and Diego both. That's all I wanted to do."

"*Tesoro*," he whispers. "Shh, *amore mio*."

"I was so afraid I was going to lose one or both of you. If Diego didn't sacrifice you, Genovese would kill him. Or you would. If Diego sacrificed you, I l-lost you." I shudder at the reminder, pressing my face to Rafe's shoulder as more tears spill down my face. "I can't lose you. *Il mio cuore era per te. Senza di te la mia vita non ha senso.*" My heart was meant for you. Without you, my life has no meaning.

"Then marry me, Amalia," he says, his lips at my ear. "Let me spend the rest of my life cherishing the gift you give me and the honor you do me. Let me love you the way you deserve to be loved, *mi reinita*. I swear to you, no one will come for you again. No one will hurt you. No one will dare. You're mine to protect and I won't fail you again."

"You never failed me, Rafe. *Never*," I whisper vehemently.

"Say yes, *amore mio*. I'll sign whatever you want me to sign to protect your fortune."

"I don't care about the fortune," I say. He can have it. What Alvise left me and Diego will last me for a lifetime. Besides, it's not like Rafe is hurting for the money anyway. He's a billionaire. The Cerrito fortune is probably a drop in the bucket compared to what he and his brothers have amassed in the last twenty years.

Rafe sweeps me up in his arms and carries me to the bed. He lays me out in the center before following me down. His body brackets mine, caging me in. "Tell me," he growls, impatient and grumpy. "What do I have to do to get you to agree, *tesoro*? Whatever it is, I'll do it."

"*Baciami*," I whisper. *Kiss me.*

Triumph blazes in his eyes, turning them molten. He dips his head, claiming my lips in a scorching kiss.

Heat rolls over me like a wave, setting my blood on fire for this man all over again. Just that easily, the trauma of the last twenty-four hours loosens its grips...and falls away.

"Rafe," I breathe against his lips, twining my arms around his neck. "I don't want to fight anymore." I don't need to fight. He doesn't need to either. He's already earned my submission. I've already surrendered to him. Completely.

He groans my name, shuddering on top of me.

"*Te amo*," I moan as he slips my panties to the side, filling me in one deep thrust. "*Te amo*."

"*Sei la mia vita*," he whispers back. I know he means it. I am his life.

And he's mine.

My king.

My world.

My everything.

FIVE YEARS LATER

"What do you think?" I ask, glancing at my brothers, Diego, and Mattia. We're cloistered together in the corner of the dining room, discussing our options. "Can we take them?"

They eye me sideways, doubt hanging heavy in the air around them. I can practically smell the defeat wafting from them. They don't think we can win this war. They've given up. For a long moment, no one says anything though. No one wants to be the one to break the news to me. They glance at each other, waiting for someone else to step up and deliver the blow.

Mattia cracks first. "They're killing us man," he says, his lip curling in disgust. "It's time to admit defeat, Rafe."

"True story," Gabe agrees, reaching for his beer. He

peers around Mattia, staring at the cards spread across the table in rife suspicion. "I think they're cheating."

"They aren't cheating," Nico says. "They're just fucking smarter than we are."

Luca snorts. "They aren't smarter than we are. Coda just sucks at giving us hints." He glances at me, frowning. "Does everything boil down to murder and the mafia to him?"

I shrug. "The man knows what he knows."

Mattia snorts. He doesn't disagree though. We both know he can't.

"I vote we put anyone other than Coda in charge of clues next time," Diego says, raising his voice so it carries to Coda. "I still don't know how the fuck Gambino Bambino relates to anything on that fucking board."

"Seconded," Luca says immediately.

"Motion passed," Mattia agrees.

Coda flips them off from his seat at the table, laughing quietly. "I'd like to see any of you do any better," he calls out. "Assholes."

Nico was right. The girls are smarter than we are. How the hell they're beating us at a goddamn spy game though, I don't know. Aside from him, every man in this room is a Made man. We've sworn our oaths and we all live by the same code. Our wives don't. Aside from Luca's wife, none of them grew up in this world. We should be mopping the floor with them right now.

Instead, they're one card away from victory...and we're one card from total annihilation. Literally. We've got one damn agent uncovered. The board is an uninterrupted sea of blue.

They're kicking our asses.

"Time's up," Amalia announces.

We all turn to find them watching us from their side of the table, matching looks of amusement on their faces. They know they have us beaten, and they're loving every minute of it. It's impossible to be mad about it when they're as cute as they are. Amalia's grinning from ear to ear, her hand on her belly. Her bump is only just beginning to show. Norah's practically dancing in her chair in excitement. Luca and Gabe's wives are arm in arm, fighting laughter. Mattia's wife is quieter, more subdued, but she's smiling too. Diego's wife is on the opposite side of the table beside Coda, playing spymaster for their team.

It's odd. Five years ago, my family was broken. This house was a mausoleum exactly like Amalia called it, cold and devoid of life. Nico never stepped foot through the door. Neither did Gabe if he could avoid it. Luca spent as little time here as he could too. Now, they never seem to leave. Our family is bigger than it ever was before, stronger than it ever was. I know I have Amalia to thank for that.

She refused to rest until she stitched us back together again. It wasn't easy. We've all had our own shit to deal with over the years. We've all had our own journeys to make. There have been battles to fight and wars to win and a thousand problems along the way. But somehow, we've managed to face them together.

Nico and I are good now. We aren't perfect and I

doubt we ever will be. He is who he is and I am who I am. But we understand each other. He knows that I do the things I do to protect this family. He doesn't have to agree with them. He doesn't even have to like them. But I made my choice a long time ago. I made it again when I asked Amalia to marry me. It's different this time though. I'm not playing by my father's rules anymore. This time, I'm making my own.

I'm not sure that Diego will ever entirely forgive me for killing Dario, but he's Amalia's family, and that makes him part of my family. It took a long time for me to learn to trust him with her. I still keep an eye on him just in case he ever decides he wants to start talking to the FBI again. If that day comes, well, we'll cross that bridge then. But I think that's in the past now.

Like the rest of us, he's had his own shit to deal with. He's had to make his own tough decisions. To save his wife, he realized just how far he was willing to go. It changed him. Love has a way of doing that.

It certainly changed me. I'm not the same man I was before Amalia. I'll never be him again. I'm still not one worthy of her and I probably never will be. No one will ever deserve her as far as I'm concerned. But she's mine, and I work my ass off every day to be someone she can be proud to call hers.

I'm still the man this city fears...but everyone knows the only ones who really need to worry are the criminals. It's their necks that feel the weight of my boot. I don't hurt innocent people. I guess I do have a few moral absolutes after all.

These days, my job isn't difficult. After I killed

Genovese and left half of his enforcers piled on his son's doorstep, no one else was stupid enough to come after Amalia. Once word got around that she was the long-lost Cerrito *principessa*, and that she was my new wife... well, those who remained loyal to her family had no problem swearing their allegiance to the Cerrito-Valentino dynasty.

I'm not saying there weren't problems. There were a fucking ton of those. But we handled them. We'll continue to handle them. I have a queen to protect, and two little girls who look just like her. Soon, I'll have a son too. No one will threaten my family. My father tried the eye for an eye route. It didn't work out. So I'm not doing that. I'm making them untouchable.

"What's your guess?" Norah demands.

Everyone looks to Nico and his brain for the answer.

"I hate this fucking game," he mutters, making me laugh. He doesn't know.

"Grace," I say.

Coda grins.

"Holy shit," Diego says, gaping when Coda picks up the red card and places it over the codeword, indicating that I was correct. "He got it right."

My team gapes at me.

"What was our last clue?" I ask quietly.

"Gambino bambino," Mattia says.

"Card."

Coda's smile grows.

"Holy shit," Gabe whispers.

"How could you possibly know that?" Diego demands.

"Carlo Gambino, the first boss of the Gambino family worked with Meyer Lansky to control gambling in Cuba," I say. "Gambling was his baby. Gambino bambino."

"Jesus Christ," Luca mutters. "You're like a goddamn encyclopedia of mob shit."

"Next clue?" I ask, ignoring him.

"Weapon two," Coda says, indicating there are two on the board.

I run my gaze over the board, quickly picking out the only two logical answers. "Nut and orange."

"Whoa," Norah whispers to Amalia when Coda covers the words with red cards, proving me correct. "Your husband is Murder Batman."

"No," Amalia says, her eyes soft as they meet mine across the table. Her proud smile turns my dick to steel, and I know it'll be a long night once everyone leaves. "He's not. He just refuses to lose."

"Rafe," Amalia moans, her nails in my chest and her head thrown back as she rides me. Her tits bounce, her ass landing in my lap with a loud slap on each downward strike. She looks like a goddess writhing above me, taking her pleasure from me. "God, Rafe."

"Harder, Amalia," I growl, smacking her ass when she lifts off. "I want you to feel me when you breathe tomorrow, *amore mio*."

She will anyway. I can't ever control myself when I'm inside her. I feel that tight cunt wrapped around my cock, and I lose my mind. It's been five years, and it's the exact same way every time. My wife owns me. I'm more obsessed with her today than ever. I'm more in love with her than ever. She's the center of my universe.

"I don't..." She trails off on a gasp. "Don't take orders from you."

The hell she doesn't. In this bed, she's mine to command.

I growl and slide her off me, flipping her carefully to her knees. I place a pillow under her stomach to protect her pregnant belly, and then lift her hips high in the air. She's only four months along, but I'm always careful with my babies. My hand comes down on her ass in a hard smack.

"Jerk," she growls, rocking back for more.

"You fucking love it." I slam myself inside her.

We both moan.

"Do not," she lies, fucking with me, trying to make

me prove it. I'm not sure which of us loves it more. Her? Me?

*Both of us*, I decide, pounding into her. I thrust my hand into her hair, craning her head back to claim her mouth in a hard kiss. "You can't live without this dick, Amalia," I growl into her mouth. "You live for it, *amore mio*."

I certainly live for her. For moments like this, when I'm inside her, fucking my way into her soul. And for the moments after, when she's lying quietly in my arms, the sweat cooling on our bodies. I live for every moment with her. For every fiery word from her mouth, and every adoring look. I live for *her*, period. And for our kids.

Without them, my life has no meaning.

"No," she moans. "I live for you, Rafe."

"*Amore mio*," I whisper, turning her in my arms.

I sit on the edge of the bed with her in my lap, her legs wrapped around my waist. She twines her arms around my neck. Our lips meet in a languid, adoring kiss. I lift her up and down my cock, making love to her slowly, sweetly, keeping her wrapped up in me.

We fall over the edge together, finding completion in unison. I hold her close to my heart, unraveling with her. Unraveling for her. Giving her every little piece of myself.

"*Te amo, mi reinita*," I whisper, pressing reverent kisses into her hairline, trailing them down the side of her face. "*Te amo*."

"Then love me again, my king," she demands, already moving on top of me again, already eager for more. Fuck, she's perfect in every way. "Make me yours. *Te amo*."

"You're already mine," I remind her.

She lifts her head, her mocha eyes radiant with happiness, her smile blinding. "I know. But I like it when you remind me."

I don't tell her no. I never do.

If you enjoyed Wrecked, please consider leaving a review! I appreciate them so much!

Are you ready to take a wild ride with the Silver Spoon MC series? The next book in the series, The Heir, releases May 3rd!

Next up from me is Crash into You, a steamy full-length instalove romance featuring an alpha cop and an unwitting murder suspect!

## The Heir

SILVER SPOON MC

**Can a billionaire biker and his rival's curvy little sister find forever together...or is blood really thicker than water?**

### Andreas Romano

Thanks to my father's shady business practices, my life has devolved into putting out one fire after another.

The latest? Dealing with the rival MC he hired to strong-arm federal regulators into looking the other way.

The Hell's Vipers have been nothing but trouble.

Until I stumble across Catriona Grady, their VPs curvy little sister.

Her bright eyes and sweet smile are pure sunshine.

But falling for her promises nothing but trouble for me and my MC.

I guess it's a good thing I've never been one to run from a fight.

Because this little light is mine.

**Catriona Grady**

People always say blood is thicker than water, but they forget the rest of that saying.

My older brother may have raised me, but he's been nothing but trouble.

He treats me like property, and I'm not interested in being owned.

Until I run into his enemy, Andreas Romano.

When Andreas touches me, I come undone.

I'm falling hard for the gorgeous billionaire.

But there's no way my brother will let him have me without a fight.

It's time to choose my side.

Family...or forever?

These wealthy Texans have it all—Money, looks, power, their MC, and brothers. The only thing missing is someone to share it all with. There's a shortage of eligible ladies in town but these determined men won't let that slow them down. These MC brothers are going to turn the town of Silver Spoon Falls, Texas, on its ear looking for their curvy soulmates.

Beginning in February 2022, Nichole Rose and Loni Ree are bringing you the Silver Spoon MC and this isn't your typical MC romance series. Nichole and Loni like to keep things light. Come along with us on this wild instalove ride.

*The Heir is available for pre-order.*

# Crash Into You

**This curvy teacher never anticipated being charged with murder...or falling for the bossy detective in charge of the case.**

### Ivy Kendall

Cameron Lewis is the man of my dreams.

Bossy, gorgeous, and fiercely intelligent.

When he touches me, I go up in flames.

There's only one problem.

He's a homicide detective.

And I'm the primary suspect in a murder I didn't commit.

I could lose everything, and so could Cam.

But whoever is trying to ruin my life doesn't get to destroy his too. I won't allow it.

One way or another, I will stop them from harming the man I love.

Even if it means sacrificing myself.

## Cameron Lewis

Ivy Kendall thinks she's a fierce tiger.

I know she's a harmless little kitten.

She's also quickly becoming the center of my world.

But nothing is ever simple.

Someone is trying to frame her for a crime she didn't commit.

The closer we get to the truth, the more complex it grows.

Clearing her name will free her.

But learning the truth may destroy her.

I can't let that happen.

I'll protect her, no matter the cost.

*Crash Into You* is an extra steamy full-length romance featuring a homicide detective and a curvy kindergarten teacher. If you enjoy sassy heroines, OTT protective men, and steamy mysteries, you'll love this gripping romance from Nichole Rose and Ayden K. Morgen!

*Crash Into You is available for pre-order.*

**The Instalove Book Club is now in session!**

Get the inside scoop from your favorite instalove
authors, meet new authors to love, and snag freebies
and bonus content from featured authors every month.
The Instalove Book Club newsletter goes out once per
week!

Join now to get your hands on bonus scenes and brand-
new, exclusive content from our first six featured
authors.

Join the Club: http://instalovebookclub.com

**Sign-up for the mailing list to stay up to date on all new releases and for exclusive ARC giveaways from Nichole Rose.**

**Want to connect with Nichole and other readers? Join Nichole's Book Beauties group on Facebook!**

# Her Alpha Series

# *Her Bride Series*

## HIS FUTURE BRIDE

His Stolen Bride
His Secret Bride
His Curvy Bride
His Captive Bride
His Blushing Bride
His Bride: The Complete Series

# Standalone Titles

A TOUCH OF SUMMER

His Christmas Miracle
Black Velvet
Easy Ride
Falling Hard
Bossy Pants
Taken by the Hitman
His Secret Obsession
Dirty Boy
Wicked Saint
Model Behavior
Physical Science
Learning Curve
Naughty Little Elf
Angel Kisses
Romancing the Cowboy
Easy Surrender (coming soon)
Crash into You (full length)

# Claimed Series

POSSESSING LIBERTY

Teaching Rowan
Claiming Caroline
Kissing Kennedy
Claimed: The Complete Series

**Love on the Clock Series**
Adore You
Hold You
Keep You
Protect You
Love on the Clock: The Complete Series

# The Billionaires' Club

## THE BILLIONAIRE'S BIG BOLD WEAKNESS

The Billionaire's Big Bold Wish
The Billionaire's Big Bold Woman
The Billionaire's Big Bold Warrior (coming soon)

## Playing for Keeps
CUTIE PIE

Ice Breaker
Ice Prince

**The Second Generation**
A Blushing Bride for Christmas
Heartthrob (Have a Heart Charity Anthology)

# Silver Spoon MC

## THE SURGEON

The Heir (coming soon)

**writing with Loni Ree as Loni Nichole**
Zane's Rebel (coming soon)

# About Nichole Rose

Nichole Rose is a short romance author on the west coast. Her books feature headstrong, sassy women and the alpha males who consume them. From grumpy detectives to country boys with attitude to instalove and over-the-top declarations, nothing is off-limits.

Nichole is sure to have a steamy, sweet story just right for everyone. She fully believes the world is ugly enough without trying to fit falling in love into a one-size-fits-all box.

When not writing, Nichole enjoys fine wine, cute shoes, and everything supernatural. She is happily married to the love of her life and is a proud mama to the world's most ridiculous fur-babies.

You can learn more about Nichole and her books at her website or by liking her on Facebook or following her on Twitter and Instagram.

Printed in Great Britain
by Amazon